A BEND IN THE LANE

JULIE C. ROUND

OLDSTICK BOOKS

First published in 2018 by
Oldstick Books
18 Wiston Close
Worthing BN14 7PU

Copyright © 2018 Julie C. Round

Names, characters and related indicia are
copyright and trademark. Copyright © 2018 Julie C. Round

The author's rights are fully asserted. The right of Julie C. Round to
be identified as the author of this work has been asserted by her in
accordance with the Copyright, Designs and Patents Act 1988

A CIP Catalogue of this book is available from
the British Library

Paperback ISBN: 978-1-9996334-0-0

All rights reserved; no part of this publication may be reproduced, stored
in a retrieval system, or transmitted, in any form or by any means,
electronic, mechanical, photocopying, recording or otherwise, without
the prior written permission of the publisher. Nor be circulated in any
form of binding or cover other than that in which it is published and
a similar condition including this condition being imposed on the
subsequent purchaser.

All the characters in this book are fictitious.
Any resemblance to actual persons, living or dead,
is entirely coincidental.

Front cover image:
Wolfgang Zwanzger | Shutterstock.com

chandlerbookdesign.com

Typeset in Adobe Garamond Pro 12pt by
www.chandlerbookdesign.com

Printed in Great Britain by
4Edge Limited

Also by Julie C. Round

Lane's End

Un-Stable Lane

The Third Lane

Never Run Away

Never Pretend

A Lesson for the Teacher

To the Sea Scribes with thanks for their help,
encouragement and friendship.

ONE

'Nan, do you mind? I want to go to Australia.'
Rose Smith stared at her grandson.

'Robbie? When did you have this idea?'

'I've been thinking about it for weeks. Now Shep has died I need to train up the new dog so I think it's the right time. I haven't done anything about it yet. I want to travel and see the world before I get too old.'

'Too old! You're only twenty three.'

'But there's so much I haven't seen or done. I've got into a rut. I have to try now.'

'But it's so far away.'

Even as she spoke Rose knew she understood what her grandson was saying. She felt a wave of sympathy.

In her youth she, too, had felt the urge to explore. That is why she had bought a caravanette and travelled round southern England – but there was more involved with Robbie. He had been a late developer, more interested in animals than people, and although he'd found a career he loved, as a shepherd in Wales, it did seem as if he had grown old before his time.

It was almost ten years since Robbie had left his first cross-country race to stop and tend to an injured sheep. The incident had shaped the rest of his life.

When Rose had discovered her cousins on her mother's side living and working in Wales it had seemed the ideal solution for both of them to move to the farm, Robbie to tend sheep and Rose to help in the shop for the caravan park.

As she had spent her years since selling her cottage in a camper van she had been content to spend her retirement in a static mobile home.

'This isn't because of a girl, is it?' she asked.

'No, of course not. The Evans' children may be into all that social stuff but I have never wanted to spend time with crowds of people and I can't understand why they would want to stare at a tiny screen all day.'

'But you do use a computer.'

'Yes, and that's why it doesn't matter how far away I go from you. There's ways of seeing people you are talking to. You'll need a laptop, Nan. You'll probably see more of me than you do now.'

'What does your mother think?'

'I'm not asking her. I'll tell her when I've decided where I'm going. Thanks for the scones, Nan. I'll see you tomorrow.'

Rose watched him stride away from her mobile home. He deserves some excitement in his life, she thought. Shepherding at such a young age was OK but he'd had no experience of life away from Wales. She'd miss him, but maybe he was right. Maybe she, too, had switched off from life too early. Perhaps there were experiences left for her to enjoy.

If he was going travelling it might do her good to do something similar – not to Australia, of course, but there were still places in the UK she hadn't seen.

There would be nothing to keep her here once he had left. The caravan site was closed for the winter. The Evans's could manage the shop for the few hours a week it was open for the remaining residents.

She supposed she hadn't thought of it before because she was on her own. Trips out always seemed more fun with someone to share things with - but there were coach trips that meant everything was arranged, weren't there? It would be something worth looking into.

Suddenly Robbie's news did not seem such a disaster. Maybe it would not be for her, but what would Katie, his mother, say, when she knew?

The next day she went into the village and searched through the shelves in the newsagent's.

'Can I help you, Rose?' asked the assistant. 'Are you looking for anything special?'

'Oh, thank you, Cathy. Actually, I was looking for coach holidays.'

'You'll have to go on line for those, or order a brochure. There is one magazine that has a few in the back – look, here it is. If you go with them everyone will be about the same age.'

Rose blushed. 'I'm probably too old to start now,' she said.

'Never say never, Rose. My Gran went to Edinburgh for the Tattoo and loved it.'

'Really?'

'She said there's loos on the coach and they stop at really nice hotels. Give it a try. I'll get the details for you.'

'There are places I'd like to go,' murmured Rose to herself, 'before it's too late.'

She flicked through the magazine the assistant had given her, wishing she had not been so afraid of getting a computer. There hadn't seemed to be any reason to have one. Although her family were spread around the British Isles she could phone them, and write letters.

Bernard, her son-in-law, was the one who liked emails, while her daughter was content to use old fashioned methods of keeping in touch.

She would have to ring Katie to find out what she thought of her son's idea about moving to Australia. Katie would probably encourage him, she thought. Her daughter had always seemed fearless to her – for defying her father, to choosing to marry a man with learning difficulties, to fighting to stop her daughter Heather being adopted.

It had not been easy for Katie, especially when Social Services had suggested that Bernard was not capable of looking after his daughter while Katie was at work, but once Rose had offered to have the whole family to live with her at Lane's End everything slotted into place, at least until the floods threatened to ruin their home and their livelihood.

Then the Garden Centre purchased the smallholding and Katie's family moved to 10 the Meadows. Katie took up chiropody and, as the children moved out, let two of the bedrooms to holiday makers.

Rose was proud of Katie.

Bernard and Katie's house at The Meadows was on the edge of a village on the South Downs.

Bernard worked part-time at the local Garden Centre and carved decorative animals and furniture in his spare time.

His poor hearing and his slow thinking had not prevented him from having a life that was happy and fulfilling. Being tall and strong he found it satisfying to take a local group of disabled people on holidays.

'It's like when I helped Zak at the college. Lifting him in and out of his wheelchair and helping him get dressed,' he explained to Katie.

'But Zak was clever, and he helped you, too,' she said. 'It must be more difficult with people who cannot speak.'

'You just get to understand what they want after a while – it's just a feeling.'

'Well, I think you're amazing - and it certainly does you good to get away and visit other places. Talking of which, Robbie rang me yesterday. He's planning to go to Australia.'

'Isn't that on the other side of the world?'

'Yes, but there are opportunities for a shepherd. He wouldn't seem so far away if we used the internet.'

'You didn't try to stop him?'

'No. It's his life. He was already away from us in Wales.'

'Is it safe?'

'Oh, Ned. It's quite civilised. It's just that there are lots of sheep.'

'That explains it. He always did prefer animals to people.'

'The person I'm worried about is Nan. She's going to miss him dreadfully. I think we should invite her to stay for a while.'

'That will be nice.'

'Well, we don't have any guests in November or over Christmas so once the Grangers have left there will be two empty bedrooms. She can have her pick.'

'Mrs Granger is funny. She wanted to know why you call me Ned when my name is Bernard.'

'Oh, not that old story again. I suppose you told her about the old lady in the houseboat who got your name wrong and you were too shy to correct her.'

'I quite liked being Ned the artist. It made me feel important.'

'Well, it was Ned I fell in love with and I'm not calling you anything else now, unless I'm very cross with you. I must go. I have to do Mrs Bright's feet at ten o'clock. I'll be back at lunchtime and we can decide what to do about my mother.'

Rose had ordered a number of holiday brochures from firms who did coach tours. She was impressed by the variety of places she could visit, from Gardens in Cornwall to Hadrian's Wall.

However, there was one place she had set her heart on for her first trip. Years ago Bernard and Katie had taken Heather to Blackpool to see the lights.

Rose hadn't been able to go but it had seemed such a happy time she'd promised herself to visit the town herself, one day.

After the move to Wales she'd forgotten all about it. She'd felt as if she had settled into a peaceful retirement, her only activity helping out at the caravan site owned by her relatives, the Evans'.

Now, with her grandson leaving, she realised her life was going to be very dull unless she did something about it. 'Seventy five is the new fifty five,' she told herself. It was October and the holiday shop could do very well without her. There were only six residential vans and the Evans' would not need the extra help until the following Easter. She was free to go wherever she liked and the five day trip to Blackpool looked the perfect choice.

Katie's letter arrived a few days later and Rose was relieved, but not surprised, to see that she had accepted Robbie's decision.

'Please reassure him that I think it is a good idea but he must keep in touch with us and come and see us before he leaves,' she wrote.

This was followed by an invitation to Rose. She smiled. Now she had begun to plan her trip she felt more like travelling. She no longer drove but she could go on the Blackpool holiday and then visit her daughter for Christmas.

There had been one seat left on the coach trip when she booked it. She hoped she would be sitting next to someone nice.

Life was beginning to get more exciting all the time. Now she had to convince Katie she hadn't gone mad. If this trip proved enjoyable she fully intended to do some more. She'd better have her hair done and shop for a new outfit. Her brown curls had turned into salt and pepper and she liked going for a set. She wanted to look good for Blackpool.

TWO

Rose found she was a little nervous as she waited to board the coach. The vehicle looked quite new. It had a brown and cream livery and had a recent number plate. That was reassuring.

The seats were brown, with little cream curtains tied back from the windows.

Behind each seat was a pocket with a brown paper bag and some literature about the company. She hoped there would be a map of their journey but doubted it, as the vehicles were used for so many different holidays.

Who would be on the seat next to her? Would it be someone who needed to talk or someone who didn't speak her language? She wasn't sure which would be worse.

She stumbled down the coach looking for her seat number. She knew it was next to the aisle.

When she found it she was surprised to see the seat by the window was occupied by a child. It was a boy of about seven and he was kneeling up, looking over the back of the seat at two adults, presumably his mother and father.

Rose sat down with her handbag on her lap. She had brought her largest one as it had to hold her spare glasses, her purse, her gloves, her phone, a magazine, tissues and a packet of her favourite fruit pastilles. Her new wheeled case was under the coach where the driver had stored it.

'Sit down, properly, Ollie,' said the young woman in the seat behind him.

The boy responded by turning round and bumping his behind into the seat saying,   'When are we going to go? I want to start.'

Neither of the adults looked at Rose. She felt the familiar invisibility of the old. Should she speak to the child or ignore him? Would he like to play a game, like I Spy, as she had done with Katie when she was young, or didn't children do that nowadays?

They seemed to spend all their time looking at screens – but Ollie didn't seem to have one with him. He was rubbing at the window with his sleeve and swinging his legs so that his feet struck the seat in front of him.

'Go, go, go – poo, poo, poo,' he chanted, with a sideways look at Rose to gauge her reaction.

Rose ignored him and lowered her eyes to her bag. She would not reward him with attention.

'I'm hungry,' he announced in a loud voice.

'You can't be,' said his mother. 'You've just had breakfast.'

At that he swivelled to his knees again and looked over the back of the seat.

'Dad – Can I use your phone?'

'No. There's no signal.'

'Can I have a drink?'

'No. Sit down.'

'Can I change places?'

'No, you wanted a window seat. You can swap with your mother after lunch.'

'Why aren't we going?'

'Not everyone is here yet.'

'I don't want to sit here' (with a sideways look at Rose.)

'Here, have my phone, but please be careful with it. You know where the games are.'

Gleefully the boy sat tapping the keys. Rose reached into her bag for her magazine.

The door of the coach closed and the driver stood facing them.

'Good morning, ladies and gentlemen,' he began. 'My name is Trevor and I'll be your driver for the holiday. Today we will be stopping at Chester for one hour for lunch and then joining the M6 on our way to Blackpool. There will be a short stop at a service station on the way and we should arrive in plenty of time for dinner. There are toilet facilities by the midsection exit. There is no smoking on the coach. Any questions?'

'What's the weather in Blackpool?' came a voice.

Trevor laughed. 'Dry and sunny,' he said. 'Real seaside weather, but a bit cold for a dip.'

There was a murmur of amusement from the passengers and Trevor sat down and started the engine.

Ollie wriggled in his seat and Rose hoped he didn't want to get out and use the toilet. She'd have liked to be next to the window but she was glad they were stopping at Chester.

She had a pen in the bottom of her bag. Perhaps she could try the crossword in her magazine.

The little screen kept Ollie amused for about ten minutes and then he was looking over the back seat again.

'Have you got my car?' he asked.

'Yes,' replied his mother. 'But you can't play with it here.'

'I can. I just want to hold it.'

The toy was handed over and the boy sat down. He span the wheels of the car and then drove it up the window and across the top of the seat in front of him.

A white haired lady turned round and smiled at him.

'Be careful, love. If it comes over the side you'll lose it.'

Maybe it was the way she looked him straight in the eyes or maybe it was the tone of her voice – but Ollie seemed to hear the threat behind the remark and crawled down into the space between the seats and drove it over the place where he had been sitting, making engine noises all the while.

'Get up, Ollie,' growled his father. 'Look out of the window. Behave yourself.'

Ollie scowled and sat back up, shooting a glance at Rose as he did so.

'What's your name?' he asked.

'Rose, like the flower.'

Ollie snorted.

'Are you very old?'

'Older than your mum and dad.'

'Are you going to die?'

'One day, but not on this trip, I hope.'

'You smell funny.'

'That's my perfume. Don't you like it?'

'Why do ladies have perfume?'

Rose blushed. This conversation was getting embarrassing.

'I suppose it's because we like to smell like the flowers,' she replied.

'I hate flowers,' he declared.

'What do you want to be when you grow up?' Rose said, changing the subject.

'A racing car driver. My Dad has a Porsche.'

'Is that a fast car?'

'Yes, faster than this stupid coach.' He turned and looked over the back of the seat. 'When are we getting there, Mum? I'm bored.'

'Why don't you see how many red cars you can count,' she said, tiredly.

'I'm on the wrong side of the coach. It's all houses.'

'How about a game?' said Rose. 'Do you know your alphabet?'

'Of course – abcd...'

'OK. What you do is this. I'll start -I went to the shop and I bought- and I have to think of something beginning with A.'

'Apple.'

'Yes, but it's my turn. Then you say- I went to the shop and I bought an apple and something beginning with B.'

'A banana?'

'Good. I went to the shop and I bought an apple, a banana and a carrot. Now it's your turn.'

Ollie smiled. 'I went to the shop and I bought an apple, a banana, a carrot and a dinosaur!' he exclaimed in triumph.

Rose laughed. 'That's a good one,' and they went on playing until she could see Ollie was struggling so she gave up and let him win.

The game seemed to have tired him out and he curled up in a ball and went to sleep with his head on her arm.

Rose let her eyes close. Perhaps she, too, could have a little nap.

The coach driver recommended a nearby restaurant in Chester but Rose wandered down the main street marvelling at the black beamed architecture and the upper level shops. She found a small café where she ordered Welsh rarebit and a pot of tea and purchased a carton of apple juice and a couple of flapjacks for later.

To her relief Oliver's father had bought him some comics to look at for the rest of the journey and it was an uneventful ride into Blackpool.

The hotel was a few streets back from the front. The foyer was quite dark, the only bright lighting being behind the reception desk.

I wouldn't like to try to read in here, thought Rose.

The regency striped wallpaper looked tired and old fashioned and the carpet showed signs of wear. Too many cases trundling across it, she decided. It's a pity they didn't change it for vinyl.

However, the receptionist had a broad smile and a soft northern burr. She booked Rose in and directed her to the lift.

Rose had been given a small first floor room with its own bathroom and a window looking out over the extensive garden.

I'll have to get some postcards as soon as possible, she thought, or I'll be home before they get there.

As she hung her clothes in the wardrobe she considered what to wear for the first dinner. She wouldn't go downstairs in the trousers she'd worn for the journey, but it didn't seem special enough for her new dress.

She decided on a navy skirt and floral blouse. The hotel was quite hot. She didn't need a jacket or a cardigan.

Unfortunately, when Rose entered the dining room she found most of her fellow travellers seated at tables of four or two, with the only spaces on Oliver's table or an empty table in the corner set for two.

Hesitantly, and hoping Oliver's family would not feel insulted, she sat down at the small table and picked up the menu.

She was still reading it when a warm masculine voice interrupted her.

'Excuse me,' he said. 'Do you mind if I join you? I hate dining alone.'

Rose looked up. The gentleman was white haired, very upright and smartly dressed in a blazer and grey trousers. He had a neat moustache and rimless spectacles and she didn't want to stare but she thought his eyes were blue.

'I'd be delighted,' she replied. 'Are you on the coach? I'm sorry, I didn't see everybody.'

'Oh, no. I'm not part of your trip. In fact, this is my hotel – or rather, one of them. Major Trent,' and he held out his hand.

'Rose Smith,' she mumbled as she shook his hand. 'One of the many.' Why did she always seem to apologise for her name? She felt herself blushing.

'How charming,' responded her companion as he sat down. 'And what did you fancy, tonight, Rose?'

'I hadn't really finished looking. What do you recommend?'

'The liver and bacon is the healthy option but I like the salmon croute. Do you drink wine?'

Rose was getting flustered. This was quite unexpected - almost like a date.

'Not tonight, I think,' she answered. 'The journey was rather tiring. It might go to my head.'

'Fine, then I'll order some water. Would that suit? Now, a starter or a sweet?'

'The fish and a fruit salad would be perfect. Do you live here all the time?'

'Oh no, only the first part of the winter.' He motioned to the waiter. 'I'd like to order now, please, George.'

'Certainly Major. I'll be right with you.'

Rose couldn't remember an evening going so quickly. Eventually it seemed like a blur. She accepted a fancy coffee and staggered up the short flight of stairs to her room, her eyes heavy and her mind in a fog.

Had she made a fool of herself? Had she told a stranger too much? Did he think she was boring? Did he actually own the hotel or just live there?

She couldn't remember what they had talked about and got ready for bed in a daze. It was years since she'd had dinner with a man. She hadn't really noticed what she was eating. It had not been a relaxed experience. Tomorrow, at breakfast time, she would try to go down early and sit at a larger table. The morning was free for exploring with a choice of places to visit in the afternoon and then, after dinner, a ride on the tram to see all the lights. She was only there for three days and she didn't want any complications.

Tuesday morning there was no sign of the Major and Rose told herself to stop making such a big issue out of a casual acquaintance.

After a delicious full English breakfast she went in search of a newspaper and some postcards. Most of them were pictures of places she had not yet seen but she bought three, one of the Tower and two of the model village she intended to visit that day. The choice between that and the zoo was easy, especially as she expected Ollie's family to choose the latter.

On Wednesday night they were all due to attend the circus in the Tower Ballroom and in the afternoon they were going to visit the waxworks at Madame Tussauds. Thursday was a free day and Rose determined to book a hair appointment. She wanted to make a good impression on her final evening.

That night there was still no sign of Major Trent and the couple who had been sitting in front of her on the coach invited her to join their table. She discovered they were both retired schoolteachers and sympathised with her on having to sit with Ollie.

'You did very well,' said the lady. 'Have you had children?'

So Rose told them about her daughter, Katie and her granddaughter, Heather, who had married an injured soldier who was now a teacher in Durham.

'I wrote to them saying how much I was enjoying this trip,' she said. 'It would be easy for them to come here just for a day.'

'What did you think of the model village?'

'I found it fascinating, and so realistic.'

The couple agreed and they settled into a comfortable silence while they ate their meal. The evening was concluded with a few games of Bingo. It wasn't something Rose usually did but the company was so friendly she had an enjoyable time.

It was Wednesday afternoon before Rose saw the Major again. She had walked back from the waxworks along the front but the wind was cold and she returned to the hotel in the hope of getting a hot chocolate. The barman duly obliged and she took it into the lounge, only to find Major Trent, sitting by himself in front of the fire, reading a newspaper.

As soon as she entered he called her over and pulled a small coffee table towards them.

'Rose,' he said, 'How are you enjoying your holiday?'

'It is a bit hectic,' she said. 'I'm not used to quite so much activity.'

'You have made friends, I hope?'

'Oh yes, Mr and Mrs Douglas have taken me under their wing.'

'I do hope they will allow me to have dinner with you

on Thursday, before you leave us. I'm afraid I have been too busy to dine in every night.'

'You are very kind. I feel I am being spoilt.'

'Not at all. You can tell me everything that is right and everything that is wrong with Blackpool.'

'I haven't found anything wrong,' she replied, 'even the young girls with their short skirts and pink and blue hair seem to be having a fun time.'

'Ah – the dreaded hen nights. They are usually at the weekends. It's the stag nights that get a bit out of hand but my customers are usually all tucked up in bed by then.'

'We are really staying in your hotel, then. It's a credit to you.'

'One in Blackpool, one in Malta and one in Cornwall. Perhaps you could visit one of those, sometime.'

'I would need a new passport. My next trip could possibly be Cornwall. There's so much of these islands I have not seen.'

'What a good choice. Well, I'm afraid I must leave you again. I look forward to tomorrow. I shall not be dining in tonight. I recommend the beef bourguignon.'

He rose, gave a slight bow and left the room. Rose felt a little disappointed. Somehow she was not so unsure of herself any more. It was almost as if just starting on this adventure had given her extra confidence. I really was turning into a bit of a hermit, she thought. Not any more!

The circus that evening made her feel old and tired. The ballroom was impressive but the lights and the music were too much for someone who usually went to bed at ten o'clock. She was grateful that she had time to herself on their final day.

* * *

It was a beautiful sunny day and she sat for a while, looking at the sea wondering how much to tell her daughter. I'll just have to emphasise that he was a lonely old man, taking pity on a client on her own, she decided.

Her new dress was full length and purple with a shaped neckline that showed off her still smooth skin and long lace sleeves that clung to her arms, directing the eye away from her ample bosom. It made her stand straighter, feel taller. It was like nothing she had worn before.

She had a moment when she looked at herself in the mirror and wondered if it was too regal. After all, she was only a poor farmer's widow. But when she entered the dining room she found everybody had dressed up. There were dresses of scarlet, silver, gold and black, with plenty of jewellery on display. Rose only had some small pearl earrings. She wasn't overdressed at all.

Major Trent was already at his usual table and he stood to greet her, pulling out her chair.

'You look lovely,' he whispered as she sat down. Blushing, Rose hid her face in her menu.

Major Trent seated himself opposite her and waited until she looked up.

'I took the liberty of ordering a bottle of Rosé,' he said. 'That will go with almost everything on the menu. What would you like?'

'I think I fancy the chicken in creamed leek sauce,' she replied, 'and I'll have a starter tonight – maybe a prawn cocktail?'

'And I'll join you. I know for a fact that the chicken is

the chef's own recipe. The rosé will go perfectly with that, a rose for a Rose – would you like to try it?'

Rose nodded. 'You know a great deal about food, don't you? Was that something you did in your past?'

'One of the things. It has been a very varied career.'

'And your tie? It looks regimental.'

'How perceptive. Yes, it is the Rifles- although they were disbanded as such by the time I joined them and became part of the Special Air Service.'

'The SAS, how exciting.'

'Not really, in peacetime. I was in France for a while and then back in England to train others. We aren't encouraged to talk about it.'

'Of course. Have you any family?'

'I'm afraid not. I've never married – too busy or too selfish. I never found anyone who would put up with me – but you are fortunate enough to have children?'

'Only one, my daughter. After my husband died our smallholding was almost destroyed in a flood so I sold it and moved in with her and her husband.'

'So how did you end up in Wales?'

'That's another story. My mother was Welsh and left some gold jewellery. I wanted to find out where it came from and in doing so I found a family I didn't know about and decided to stay.'

She paused, then, as their starter had arrived. I'm talking too much, again, she thought. What would he say if he knew she lived in a mobile home?

She finished her prawn cocktail determined to put the conversational ball back in his court.

'Where do you live the rest of the year?' she asked.

'I spend four months in each hotel,' he replied. 'September to December here, January to April in Malta and May to August in Cornwall. Are you going to continue holidaying with the same company?'

'If it's as good as this, certainly. This week was just what I needed.'

'You are seeing family at Christmas?'

'Yes, I've been invited to stay with Katie. There won't be any children. I just hope my grandson won't have gone to Australia by then.'

'Well, if you get a new passport you'll be able to visit him there. It's somewhere I have never been.'

'But you do know Malta. What is it like?'

'You either love it or hate it,' he began, but their main course arrived and, once again, they turned their attention to the meal.

Rose felt comfortable, now, knowing that she did not have to keep up a conversation while eating. The silence didn't seem awkward and the chicken was as delicious as her companion had suggested.

The Major refilled her glass with a smile. 'It's an English wine, from Kent,' he said, 'Only 9%. Do you like it?'

'I don't usually drink wine,' she answered. 'This is a real treat.'

'Have you chosen a dessert?'

'I'm not sure I could manage one.'

'A little cheese, perhaps. I'll order for myself and you can share it, even if you only have the grapes.'

His laugh was a deep chuckle. She smiled in response. She was actually enjoying herself.

* * *

Next morning Rose woke with a feeling of dread. She was going to have to endure a journey home with young master Oliver. After the wonderful time she'd had it was such a pity to spoil it.

Major Trent had taken down Katie's address and promised to write to Rose at Christmas. He urged her to book her week in Cornwall as soon as possible as he knew the coach company used his hotel and he would contrive to be there when she came.

He was not at breakfast or anywhere to be seen as they loaded the coach. Then, at the last minute, he appeared with a small box wrapped in gift paper.

'For Christmas,' he said. 'Au revoir, Rose.'

She couldn't help herself – she reached up and planted a kiss on his cheek.

'Thank you,' she said, and turned to board the coach. Stumbling down the aisle she was pleasantly surprised to find Oliver's mother sat where Ollie had been.

'Thank you for entertaining Ollie on the way here,' she said. 'He's a bit spoilt, being the only one. Did you have a nice holiday?'

Rose heard the smile in her voice. They saw me kiss the Major, she thought. What the heck. It's my business, not anyone else's.

'Yes, thank you,' she said primly. 'It was very refreshing,' and sat down, opened her bag and got out her magazine.

The lunch stop on the return journey was once again at Chester but, this time, Rose went with the crowd. Mr and Mrs Douglas tried engaging her in conversation but her thoughts were elsewhere. She had just over a month to persuade Robbie to stay until the New Year. She didn't know how long it would take to arrange his departure but it was important that he spent Christmas with the family.

Katie was having similar thoughts. If she put her mother in Heather's old room Robbie could stay in his old bedroom. Of course, it didn't look the same now she had been letting it to visitors but the view of the garden was almost unchanged.

They no longer had all the animals that he had collected when he was younger – only a recent addition to the household, a fat, fluffy grey cat they had christened 'Bagpuss.'

Robbie had explained that he was going on a visit first – before he made up his mind whether he wanted to stay longer. He was in touch with a farmer who had offered him three weeks work as soon as he could travel but he didn't think he'd be ready before the end of January.

'I'll go back to Wales after Christmas and get the new shepherd settled in,' he told his mother.

'That's good, you'll be able to take your grandmother.'

But Rose had other ideas. 'If I can stay with you until Easter, when your visitors start coming again, I can book my next holiday from here,' she told Katie.

'Oh, Mum, you must have had a great time if you're already planning the next one.'

'I did. I enjoyed Blackpool immensely, although I thought I might not.'

'What was the hotel like?'

'Fine.'

'And the food?'

'Excellent.'

'And the people with you - were they friendly?'

'Very. I met a nice gentleman who I might see again.'

'Mother – you have to be careful.'

'I know. I've heard all the warnings – but he didn't ask me for anything. In fact, he's probably much better off than I am. It's his hotel I'm going to after Easter, in Cornwall, near the Eden Project.'

'You'll enjoy that. Ned and I plan to go one day. You can tell us all about it.'

'You don't mind if I stay until then?'

'Of course not. If you want to come back permanently we'd love to have you.'

'Thanks, darling. That puts my mind at rest. Now, will Bernard book my trip for me on the computer or should I ask Robbie?'

'If you're there to watch I'm sure either of them could do it. I think they are planning to get you a laptop for Christmas. Don't let on I told you.'

True enough, Rose's Christmas present was a laptop computer and she was introduced to emails and Skype.

The first people she emailed were Heather and Ryan who responded with news of their own. Heather was pregnant. The baby was due in June and they hoped Rose could come up and stay with them in the summer if she wasn't needed in Wales.

Rose couldn't believe her luck. Her whole life seemed to be changing, speeding up, taking a new direction, filling with adventures.

She'd tell the Evans's she'd return in August, for the school holidays, if required but, if Katie agreed, she might let her mobile home and move back to Sussex.

The next few days were taken up with contacting Robbie's sponsoring employer and getting a temporary visa for Australia.

Rose's holiday was booked and paid for so she settled into life at the Meadows.

CHAPTER
THREE

It didn't take Rose long for her to realise that staying with her daughter was not what she wanted. Much as she loved Katie she had been on her own for too long to be able to fit into her daughter's lifestyle. It wasn't her kitchen, she was expected to tell Katie when and where she was going when she went out. She almost felt like a guest or, worse still, a child.

It was fine for a week or two but not as a permanent arrangement. If she was going to come back to Sussex she would have to have her own home, nearby, as she used to, but, until then at least she had her holiday to look forward to.

Yet something was spoiling the anticipation. Was she hoping for too much? Did she want to see the Major again or would she rather not? The old fears of inadequacy returned. Something that should have been a pleasant memory was turning into a cause of anxiety. This was not how one should feel when preparing for a holiday.

Before she even boarded the coach she had made up her mind to go somewhere else, with a different company, next time. Perhaps she'd do a Turkey and Tinsel weekend, somewhere close, like the Isle of Wight – or perhaps Katie would come with her. There would be no meeting up with strange gentlemen then. The thought of it was making her nervous.

However, she had corresponded with Major Trent and his reply calmed her somewhat. He said he would be returning mid week and hoped he could accompany her to the Eden Project and, perhaps, have the final dinner with her as before.

Rose showed Katie the letter.

'That doesn't seem too pushy,' she said. 'What does he look like, this Major?'

'Upright, white haired with a neat moustache,' said Rose. 'He dresses smartly, with a tie, a bit old fashioned, I suppose.'

'Well that seems harmless. Just be careful.'

'You don't have to keep warning me – I'm old enough to look after myself,' she snapped and left her daughter wondering what had got into her usual placid mother.

The New Year brought news that nobody had expected. Chantelle, who was living with Bernard's father in the Lake District, rang to say James had advanced Alzheimer's and was declining fast.

'Please can Bernard come and see him as soon as possible? I can't guarantee that he'll recognise him but I had to tell you before it was too late.'

Katie sprang into action.

'Robbie, you'll have to take your father,' she commanded. 'You won't need to stay long – but it's the least we can do. I'm sorry, Ned, but he's over 80 and it does happen to a lot of people.'

'Can I take him some photographs?' asked Bernard.

'What a good idea. Tell them at the Garden Centre that I'll help in the sales if they can't manage without you. If you go on Wednesday and come back Saturday you'll miss most of the heavy traffic.'

'It'll be late when we get there, Mum,' said Robbie. 'We'll have to book into a Travelodge. I'll find one on line. Is granddad still at home?'

'Yes, but Chantelle says not for much longer. She sounds as if she can't cope. I do hope there are some good facilities up there. It's such a shame.'

Bernard left them and walked out into the garden. His father had always been a conundrum. First, he had left Bernard and his mother when he found his son had limited abilities. Then he'd come back into their lives when Heather was very young. Finally, he had taken up with Chantelle, a woman much younger than himself and they had disappeared to the Lake District as if they no longer wanted to be part of the family. Heather had been the only person to keep in touch with them.

Bernard didn't understand his father at all – but he was aware that he stirred up a mixture of emotions in him. Love was there, but so was disappointment and even anger.

Now he could no longer be angry with him – instead he supposed he should feel pity – but until he had actually set eyes on him he was just confused. He would be happy to see Chantelle again. She had always been positive and welcoming, even to helping him with his reading. That's what he would concentrate on. He was going to visit Chantelle.

'We'll have to go in my pick-up,' Robbie told his father. 'I'm not on Mum's insurance.'

'I don't mind. I'm sorry I don't drive.'

'You can help me stay awake. It's not easy going a long way on your own.'

'If Ned wants to stop, you will, won't you?' said Katie.

'Of course. I always have a break every two hours, anyway.'

They set off just after nine on Wednesday morning, stopping near Winchester and again at Warwick.

'I'll have to shut my eyes for a bit, Dad,' said Robbie. 'You go and stretch your legs.'

Bernard did as he was told and wandered round the service station hoping he could find a present for Chantelle. He wanted to buy flowers but settled on a box of chocolates. He found a key ring that was also a torch and bought it for himself. Then he bought a mug of coffee and some doughnuts. The machine delivered them in threes so he took two back to the truck.

It was getting dark and Robbie looked as if he was still asleep. Bernard wasn't sure what to do. He'd been to the toilet and looked round the shops. How much further did they have to go? They were booked into a Travelodge in Kendal. He was getting cold. He tapped gently on the window and Robbie sat up immediately.

'Thanks, Dad,' he said. 'I'll just pop in there for a minute. I won't be long.'

Bernard clambered into his seat and placed the chocolates and doughnuts on the floor.

Soon they were back on the motorway and he felt himself drifting off. The cab was warm and the sound of the engine, soothing. It was his turn to go to sleep.

Robbie woke him at another service station and they ate the doughnuts and then went inside for more coffee. Robbie made Bernard move the chocolates to his bag, hanging over the back of his seat.

'I just hope they haven't all melted,' he laughed. 'Only another hour and a half and we'll be there.'

The pick-up stopped at last at a large warehouse-type camping shop.

Chantelle was coming down some steps at the side of the building and Robbie jumped out to greet her with a hug.

'You could have waited until morning,' she said. 'I'm afraid James isn't here.

He's in a Care Home in Kendal. But do come in for a cup of tea.'

Bernard's legs felt stiff but he picked up the box of chocolates and carried them with him up to the flat above the store.

'It's lovely to see you again, Bernard,' said Chantelle.

'I bought you these,' he said, awkwardly.

'Thank you. If you don't mind I'll keep them for later,' she replied and he suddenly remembered she had problems with her weight.

He stood in the centre of the room taking in the cream coloured walls covered with paintings – landscapes, abstracts and even a portrait of Chantelle, her hair piled high and a beautiful necklace of blue stones round her neck.

'My Dad did these?' he asked.

'Of course. He didn't just paint walls and ceilings,' she giggled.

'How is he?' enquired Robbie.

'Not good. He started getting up in the night and going downstairs. I couldn't lock him in, could I? But he could get lost in the woods, or even fall in the lake. It was too dangerous. He kept calling me Anne – that was your mother's name wasn't it, Bernard?

'Yes.'

'Well, I expect you're both tired. How about a bowl of broth and some home-made bread before you go and check into your hotel – or would you rather eat there?'

'That would be great,' said Robbie. 'It will be as much as I can do to flop into bed when I get there.'

'Would you rather stay here? I can make up the couch?'

'No, thank you. It's all arranged, and it will be nearer to James. When can we see him?'

'They don't specify visiting times although I expect they would like us to avoid mealtimes. How about I meet you at the hotel at ten o'clock?'

She bustled into the kitchen. Bernard followed and stood in the doorway looking lost.

'Here, Bernard, put these on the table, would you?' said Chantelle, handing him three place-mats and spoons.

The vegetable soup was delicious and Robbie had to fight to stay awake.

'I'll make some coffee while you rest,' said Chantelle. 'Do you know where to go?'

'Oh yes, I looked it up on the computer. I've not got a satnav. I wonder if I'll need one in OZ.'

'Your Nan will miss you.'

'I know – but she might be going to live with Mum.'

'I just hope that will work out.'

Next morning, after a full English breakfast, they met Chantelle in the foyer.

'It's only a few streets away,' she said. 'What have you got there, Bernard?'

Bernard had a large black shoulder bag which he was clutching as if it held valuables.

'Photograph albums,' he said. 'Katie thought James might like them.'

'How thoughtful. Am I in them?'

Bernard smiled. 'Yes, I've looked, and the shop and Nan,'

'Well, let's hope it stirs something in James' memory.'

The Care Home was larger that Bernard had expected. It looked more like three houses turned into one, a centre building and two wings, all built of the same grey stone but with double glazed windows as evidenced by the bright white frames. The surrounding gardens were well kept although, being winter, there were few blooms to be seen. A large holly bush by the front door was covered in red berries.

Chantelle rang the bell and a young woman in a lilac overall opened the door.

'Good morning, Miss Cooper,' she said. 'Have you come to see Mr Longman?'

Bernard winced at his own name but before he could react further Chantelle took charge.

'Yes, this is his son and his grandson. Is James awake?'

'I believe so. He may still be in the dining room. If you would please wait here, I'll check.'

Bernard could hardly disguise his shock when James was wheeled out of the dining room. His tall, lean frame was shrunken and his features were hawk-like and sallow.

The trio followed him to his room where the assistant left them.

'Hallo, James,' said Chantelle. 'How are you?'

'I want to go home,' he replied.

'You will, my love, when you're better,' she soothed.

Robbie looked at Bernard. 'I didn't really know him and he won't know me,' he said. 'Can I go?'

'Where will we meet you?' said Chantelle.

'I'll see you at the hotel. I'll get my own lunch.' His eyes pleaded with them to be released.

'OK, but keep your phone on,' she said.

Bernard had turned to James. 'Look what we brought you, father,' he said.

'Who are you?'

'Bernard, Bernie, James – your son.'

'Little James? You're not little James.'

'I was a long time ago. I've got some pictures to show you, look,' and he opened the album at a picture of a cottage in the hills.

'Lane's End', he said, 'with Rose at the door. You remember Rose, and the flood? You remember helping to clear away the water?'

'Rose? And Heather?'

'That's right. When you lived in Stable Lane and sang in the pub. Where you met Chantelle. Those were good times.'

'Good times,' James repeated and, for a moment, his face seemed to brighten.

'Quick, Bernard, show him another,' said Chantelle but James' eyes had lost their focus. His concentration had gone. She sighed in frustration.

'His harmonica,' said Bernard. 'Has he still got it?'

'Not here, somewhere at home. He hasn't played in years.'

'It might help. Singing, too. What did you used to sing?'

'The Fields of Athenry, the Black Velvet Band, Always Blue, just folk songs.'

'Try one.'

'What, now?'

'Yes, go on.'

'OK. 'Her eyes they shone like diamonds ..'

They watched while James' face lit up again and he joined in.

Three songs later a nurse came bustling in.

'We need to get Mr Longman out of that chair and into bed,' she said. 'Maybe you could come back this afternoon?'

'He's on medicine for his arthritis?' asked Chantelle.

'If you want to see the doctor he will be here at three pm. Mr Longman is in good hands.'

'I don't doubt it,' said Chantelle as two assistants passed them in the doorway.

'I suppose they have to wash and shave him. I'd better get some more pyjamas. He looks so thin, poor love,' and she began to cry.

'You're doing your best, Chantelle,' said Bernard putting his arm round her. 'We must tell Heather. She'd want to know.'

'It's a cruel, cruel, disease,' she moaned. 'Let's get away from here.'

Bernard couldn't think how to cheer her up. 'You were going to choose some pyjamas,' he said, at last.

'Yes, it's the least I can do – but it hurts every time I see him. He's not going to get better, is he, Bernard?'

'He's not in pain. Let's see if we can find some music to make him happy. Robbie can take us back to the flat to fetch his harmonica – or shall we get a new one?'

'No – I think I can find it. Right, pyjamas, here we come!'

Three pm saw them back at the care home waiting to see the doctor.

The news was not good. The medication that eased James' arthritis disguised the extent of his dementia.

'He spends a great deal of his time asleep,' said the doctor, 'and when he is awake he doesn't always seem aware of his surroundings. We have tried to get him interested in puzzles or the TV but he doesn't seem able to concentrate.'

'Have you tried giving him paper and chalks?' asked Chantelle.

'Well, he wouldn't be allowed that in bed. Do you think that would help?'

'He's an artist,' said Bernard. 'It might even help his fingers.'

But when they took the new pyjamas to James he was fast asleep.

'We need to put his name in them, anyway,' said the assistant.

'We've brought his harmonica,' said Chantelle. 'Shall we leave it here?'

'I wouldn't if I were you. It might disappear. Why don't you bring it every time you come?'

Bernard bent forward and touched his father's hand. 'We'll be back tomorrow,' he said, tenderly and they left the room together.

'I wonder if they'll let me sit with him,' said Chantelle as she ushered Bernard into the flat. 'I could come every day except weekends. The store is open Saturdays and Sundays in the winter. Do you think you could stay until Monday, Bernard?'

'Of course we could,' said Robbie, coming up behind them. 'We just need to check we can have our room for an extra couple of nights.'

Bernard hadn't taken much notice of the store beneath the flat but now he realised it was an outdoor clothing and activities shop. There were rails of different coloured fleeces, tents and poles, and shelves with boxes of boots and trainers.

'We are open seven days a week from the first of March,' explained Chantelle, 'but in winter we just cater for weekend visitors.'

'It's not your shop?'

'No, we just work here. The owner has a big house by

the lake. James hasn't done much for a while but I work full time in the summer months. The previous owner let James have the flat and so they let us keep it. Now, how about staying for supper? Would a mixed grill suit?'

'We'd love to', said Bernard, 'and we'll see you tomorrow for a sing song.'

CHAPTER
FOUR

Next day Robbie had a call from Heather.

'What's happening to James?' she asked. 'Mum rang me. Have you seen him?'

'Yes. He's in a Care Home. Chantelle phoned and asked Dad to come up urgently. He's got dementia. It's horrible, Heather. I hate to see him like that.'

'We'll come over for the day on Sunday. Will you still be there then?'

'Yes, I'm sure Chantelle will be happy to see you. She's very stressed.'

'It's not surprising. How's Dad?'

'He's coping with this better than any of us. He's very patient.'

'I'll ring Chantelle and go straight to her place. We should be there late morning. Where are you staying?'

'In Kendal – not far from the Care Home. It's a good job you called now. I'm getting away from it all tomorrow.

I can't bear to watch them.'

He rang off reluctantly. Was he being selfish, hoping to take a day off on Saturday? He felt useless and needed to get out in the countryside. He intended to start from Chantelle's store, get some new sturdy walking boots and a waterproof cagoule and escape to the hills. He hated being surrounded by people, especially when they were uptight and miserable. If he had just one day of freedom he would be able to enjoy time with Heather and Ryan on Sunday.

Once out of the town and on the path over the hills Robbie began to feel better. He'd chosen a waymarked route that went up to the nearest peak so that he could experience the view of the lake.

When he got there he felt he had found where he belonged. The air was sharp and the wind keen but the scene before him made him feel warm inside. Smooth hillsides, copses of dark green trees and small flocks of sheep sheltering by rough stone walls with only the occasional habitation down by the water's edge, were his idea of heaven. But dark clouds began to chase across the sky and make shadows on the fields below. He'd heard how the mist creeps up on unwary travellers. He wasn't in the most isolated part of the Lakes but he knew it was time to make his way back.

As the wind strengthened and turned into an icy downpour the hotel no longer felt like a necessary stopping place, it became a refuge and he was glad to welcome his father when he returned.

* * *

40

'Oh, Heather, thank goodness you rang,' said Chantelle, answering her phone.

'I didn't know how to tell you. I didn't want to spoil your news and I know Ryan is back at work.'

'You should have rung before.'

'It all happened so quickly. For weeks he's been forgetful and bad tempered. Then he got extra fussy about his food and suddenly he started getting up in the night as if he thought it was morning. He got through the door at the top of the internal stairs and wandered around the store. I got him back and rang the doctor and we had to go and see him.

It was dreadful, Heather. The doctor asked him all sorts of questions about his date of birth, what month it was, who was the Prime Minister – and he couldn't get any of the answers right.

It was so obvious, and I'd been ignoring it. We went home and he got up again in the night and tried to get out of the front door. I stopped him before he could get down the steps in his pyjamas. I had to find a care home for him. I'm sorry.'

'It looks like you've done the right thing. How about legal matters?'

'We've made our wills and our solicitor has Power of Attorney. As we aren't married it seemed like the best thing at the time.'

'Good. Ryan says we'll be with you by eleven. I've got the address. Don't fret. You are doing all you can, Chantelle. We love you.'

Chantelle put down the phone. The warmth in Heather's voice had calmed her a little. She might still be

Chantelle Cooper but she felt as if she had been accepted as part of the Longman family.

Leaving Bernard with James she shopped for the weekend. Having to work was a distraction but she wished she had more time for her visitors.

The boss told her she could take Sunday afternoon off and she was determined to give everyone a roast dinner to thank them for rallying round.

Ryan and Heather drove into the car park at eleven fifteen on Sunday morning. Chantelle rushed up to greet them. Just being enfolded in Ryan's arms was a relief and Heather looked so fit and young and beautiful she had to smile.

'Being pregnant suits you,' she said. 'How was the journey?'

'Fine,' replied Heather. 'I'm not even being sick in the mornings.'

'Robbie is here in the flat. Bernard is with James. Would you like a coffee before you go on?'

'That would be great, Chantelle. We don't need any lunch. We had sandwiches on the way,' said Ryan.

'Good, because I have an early dinner planned. How long can you stay?'

'We'll have to leave by seven. Is that OK?'

'Fine, I'll see you later. It looks as if I've got customers,' and she turned towards a couple who were hovering by the rucksacks.

Although he went with them Robbie did not follow them into James' room. 'I'll wait in the visitor's lounge,' he said. 'Don't want to crowd him.'

When Bernard saw them he stood up and put his fingers to his lips.

'He's just dropped off,' he said. 'We were playing dominoes.'

'Will he remember me?' asked Heather.

'I don't know. He has his ups and downs. I don't think he knows who I am but he's happy enough when I'm here with him.'

'What time's his lunch?'

'He doesn't go down for it any more. He has it when he's awake. He doesn't eat much.'

James' eyelids fluttered. The sound of conversation seemed to have woken him.

'Who's there?' he called out.

'Heather, Dad,' said Bernard. 'You remember Heather.'

'The clever one,' said James.

A shudder went through Bernard as it came back to him, then, how James had been so ashamed of having a son with learning difficulties he had abandoned his wife and child and gone roaming about the countryside for years until a newspaper report of the sandcastle competition at Blackpool, where Heather had won a prize, alerted him to the fact that he had a granddaughter.

It was a momentous holiday, that, as Heather and Ryan had met as children and he and Katie had made friends with Ryan's parents.

The words, 'the clever one' stirred up memories of the old comparisons with Heather that reminded Bernard that James still thought of his son as flawed, inadequate, less important than his granddaughter.

He had to suppress the residual pain of rejection. After all, James was ill. He couldn't help it.

Heather stepped forward and took his hand. 'Hallo, Granddad,' she said.

'You're a pretty young lady,' said James.

'I hear you've been singing, Granddad.'

'Aye, we had a go at the Lambton Worm but I forgot the words.'

'You could play it, though, on your harmonica?'

'You'd like to hear it?'

'Yes, please.'

So James played the tune and the rest of them tried to sing along. They ended up giggling at their own incompetence but James looked happy.

'I've got Mr Longman's lunch,' said a nurse as she entered. 'He may as well have it, as he's awake.'

'Would you like me to help you, Granddad?' said Heather. 'It's chicken and stuffing. You know you like stuffing.'

Ryan stood at the door, motioning to Bernard and, once they were in the corridor began to ask about Chantelle.

'Can she manage up here by herself?' he said. 'She seems to have everything in hand. Do you think she has enough money?'

'I don't know,' replied Bernard. 'Katie deals with things like that.'

'I'll get Heather to ask her. I don't know her well enough. She seems a solid sort.'

For a moment Bernard thought Ryan was referring to Chantelle's size. He wouldn't be rude, would he? He must mean she was reliable.

Not being able to read or write until he was an adult had hampered his confidence and, as he had to concentrate just to hear what people said, he could not always think past the literal meaning of words.

It wasn't until Rose had taken him in and he had met her daughter, Katie, that he had found he was able to forge a life for himself and his family.

He'd been, 'Ned-the artist' when the old lady on the houseboat had mistaken his name and taught him about mosaics and Katie discovered he was the same person as her father had employed as 'Bernard,' at the smallholding. But when she fell in love and took 'Ned' home to meet her mother the truth had came out and, in spite of her father's opposition, she married Bernard and they had a daughter, Heather.

Bernard had become a skilled gardener and craftsman although he found reading and writing difficult. In fact, if it hadn't been for Chantelle he might never have learnt to read. She spent time in her little craft shop going over vocabulary with him.

There was so much he had to thank Chantelle for and now he felt extra grateful for the love she had for his wayward father.

The meal at the flat was extremely enjoyable. Heather and Bernard told Chantelle about the tunes they had sung with James until he began to tire and they took their leave.

Chantelle had made roast beef, yorkshire puddings, vegetables and fruit trifle. They ended the meal with coffee.

'I hate to go back and leave you,' said Heather.

'I'm fine. He's in good hands and don't worry about finances. James had his own way of providing for the future.'

Bernard remembered, then, how James had told him about the jewels that he secreted away rather than having a bank account. If he'd gone on doing that in the years he'd spent with Chantelle he'd be a rich man by now.

He and Robbie said goodbye to the Walsh's and returned to their hotel for the final night.

'I have to get back, Dad. I'm going next month.'

'I know. Perhaps Katie could come up sometime,' said Bernard. 'James does like company.'

However, when they got home everything had changed.

CHAPTER
FIVE

Chantelle looked round the empty flat after everyone had gone.

Bernard had helped with the washing up but there was still two thirds of a bottle of red wine left.

She flopped into an easy chair and sighed. It had been so good to have everyone round to help. How was she going to manage by herself?

It wasn't money she was concerned about – it was whether she would be allowed to stay in the flat on her own. If she carried on working it would probably be all right but in the summer that would leave her very little time to see James. And what if he got worse – or died?

She was too tired to think now. She finished the wine and staggered off to bed.

It was cold in the big double bed without James and when she woke in the night she felt her way to the bathroom. She had the suggestion of a headache and wondered if she should find some painkillers.

A sudden bump from below her made her pause and listen. It came again. Someone was in the shop, moving about. She grabbed for her dressing gown and tiptoed to the top of the stairs.

There was the flash of torchlight and somebody whispered something. As her eyes grew more accustomed to the gloom she could see the shapes of people, she counted three - taking clothes off the racks and passing boxes of boots and shoes out of the door to someone outside.

Without thinking, she shouted, 'Hey, stop that!' and two faces turned towards her. She was half way down the stairs and without a weapon. If her head hadn't been so muddled by the wine she might have tried to summon help. Instead, she threw herself at the nearest figure, rage blinding her to the danger.

The man fell but his companion ran towards her. He had a knife in his hand and she was unbalanced. Raising her arm to fend off her attacker she felt the blade pierce her skin, sliding down from her elbow to her wrist. As she fell backwards he struck again - the knife scraping across her chin.

'Get out of here!' shouted a voice. There was the sound of running feet, the smell of sweat and strong tobacco from the man she had knocked over as he brushed past her, a clattering sound as boxes tumbled and a slam of the door as they left. She heard an engine start up and brakes squeal as at least one vehicle moved off.

Chantelle lay still, her arm throbbing and the sensation of warm blood trickling down her neck. She knew she had to reach the phone. The nearest one was on the counter – but she felt too weak to stand.

She rolled over onto her knees and cried out as the pain from her arm intensified. Crawling forward she reached up for the phone but before she could dial she fell backwards, unconscious, knocking the phone from its cradle.

The last sound she heard was the buzzing on the line.

'I've had a call from the police at Kendal,' Katie announced, running down the path to meet them as Robbie and Bernard got out of the car.

'There was a break in at the store last night and Chantelle has been injured. She's in hospital. I don't know how serious it is and I didn't want to call you while you were driving.'

'My phone was turned off, anyway,' responded Robbie. 'What do you want to do, Mum?'

'I think you and Ned should stay here. Nan will look after you. I'll travel up tomorrow and see what I can do. I'm so sorry, Robbie. It's a real shock.'

'You shouldn't go on your own, take Dad.'

'He's got a job to go to.'

Rose rushed out of the front door in time to catch this last remark.

'Well, take Nan, then. Dad and I can look after each other.'

'What do you think, Nan?' asked Katie.

'I'd like to come. I'd like to feel I could be useful.'

'Right, that's settled. I'm sure we can stay at Chantelle's. I've given the police my mobile number. I'll call the hospital and find out how she is. What a complete disaster all this is.'

'James is OK, Mum. He's being well looked after.'

'That's something, I suppose. I'm going to the garage to fill up. Anything you need?'

'No, we can manage. Calm down. It might not be as bad as you think.'

Rose sat quiet next to Katie on the way up north. She felt chilled, as if they were going towards something fateful, something they had no control over.

It was bad enough James having dementia - but with Chantelle getting robbed and in hospital it seemed ill fortune had settled on them like a black cloud. Why was it that as soon as she felt content something happened to put them all to the test?

She'd always believed in God but it was difficult when things like this happened. She prayed that Chantelle would pull through. What else was there to hope for?

When they reached the hospital they found Chantelle sitting up in bed with a bandage round her neck and her arm in plaster.

'My dear soul,' said Rose. 'Whatever happened?'

'Hallo Rose, Katie. Thanks for coming up. I am being a real trial to your family aren't I?'

'OUR family,' said Katie, firmly. 'What does the doctor say?'

'He doesn't hold out much hope for that arm. There's no feeling in my fingers. I think I've lost the use of it. Oh, Katie, what am I going to do with only one arm?'

'Stop worrying about things you can't change,' replied Katie. 'Can we do anything to help in the flat or the shop?'

'I never thought of that. I was only thinking about James. Of course, Rose has loads of retail experience. The store was shut for one weekend but they are opening next week, now the police have finished with their investigations. I'm sure they'd love to have you to help.'

'Did they lose a lot of stock?'

'Not as much as they might have. They said I was brave but really I was foolish. If only I hadn't drunk all that wine.'

'Have the police any idea who they were?'

'They aren't telling me – but if the stock turns up at a boot fair they'll catch them.'

'Perhaps they'll sell it abroad.'

'It depends if they've done it before. I don't care. I don't want to go back there.'

'Give it time, love,' said Rose. 'Have you got the keys? We'll go and check out the flat and then go and see James tomorrow.'

'Yes, I had James' set. The police have the others. I think they're in reception. You can stay as long as you like. There's the double bed and a put-up couch.'

'Well, you get a rest. We'll report back tomorrow afternoon. Chin up, Chantelle.'

'That's a laugh,' she responded, bitterly.

When Rose and Katie reached the store the lights were on downstairs. Pushing open the doors they peered inside.

'Can I help you?' came a voice from behind a stack of shelves.

'It's Katie Longman and her mother,' said Katie. 'We are James's relatives. Chantelle said we could stay in the flat while she was in hospital. You are?'

'Guy Brown, the owner. I'm trying to get this lot ready for the weekend. We had to stock check for the insurance and now it's got to look as if nothing has happened.'

'Are you short of salespeople?' asked Rose. 'Because, if so, I'd like to help.'

'You would? If you could do half of what Chantelle did it would be wonderful. Come down tomorrow and I'll show you the ropes.'

'It will have to be in the afternoon. We are seeing James in the morning.'

'Righto. It's a pleasure to meet you. What do we call you?'

'Rose – just Rose. We'll be upstairs if you need us.'

'That's OK. I'm almost finished here. See you tomorrow, Rose.'

Rose lay awake wondering what would happen next. If Chantelle could not continue in the shop what would they do? How could she care for James if she had no job and, possibly, no home?

This was a problem that Rose could not solve on her own. They would have to take each day as it came and, meanwhile, she would have to keep busy. Maybe the young people in the family would be able to find a solution.

* * *

James was sitting with a drawing pad on his knee when Rose and Katie arrived the next morning.

Although they tried to explain who they were he didn't recognise them. Then Rose found the photograph album in the cupboard next to the bed and searched through the pictures until she found one of James by his camper van.

'Who's that, James?' she asked.

'That's me,' he said. 'When I was somewhere else.'

'Do you remember where that was?'

'Stable Lane,' he said, 'and Chantelle had a shop. Where's Chantelle? I want to go home.'

'Oh dear,' said Katie, 'We've stirred him up.'

'Are you drawing something for Chantelle?' said Rose.

'Eh?'

'Your picture.'

'I can't do it. My fingers are too stiff. I can only do sand and sea and sky.'

Sure enough, his paper had three wide horizontal stripes, blue, yellow and green.

'It looks like a flag,' said Katie. 'Very nice.'

James stared at her, an angry frown on his face.

'Where's Heather?' he demanded.

'There,' she said to Rose. 'He does know me. He associates me with Heather.'

'She's grown up, now,' said Rose. 'She's going to be a mummy herself, soon.'

But James's attention had wandered away from his visitors.

'I think he's had enough,' said Katie. 'Let's go and get some lunch.'

*   *   *

Katie went to the hospital while Rose stayed at the store. It didn't take her long to work out the system they used, the areas of stock and the till.

'If you stick to the clothing we'll do the equipment side,' said Guy Brown. 'There's a few things in a Sale basket but they're all priced.'

'What about the touristy stuff like books, maps and mint cake?' asked Rose.

'Whoever's nearest,' he replied. 'They're coming to put in CCTV, internal security cameras later on. The thieves disabled the outside one on Sunday night. There's an alarm under the counter, but I don't think it will happen again.'

It was a very tired Rose who sat opposite Katie at supper time that night.

'What did you tell Chantelle?' she asked.

'There wasn't much I could say. I did tell her James remembered the shop and Stable Lane and she seemed to think that was a good sign.'

'Did you tell her I was working in the shop?'

'Yes, but I honestly don't think she could care about that. Are you sure you can cope?'

'It's only temporary. But I think I'll have an early night. Thanks for letting me have the bed.'

With Rose working in the shop it was Katie who visited James on the Saturday.

He had no idea who she was and his breathing was laboured. She tried talking to him about the past, his paintings, Heather, anything to get a response, but he seemed in a world of his own so she gave up and leafed through the photographs that Bernard had brought.

She paused at one of Sandy, their old dog. It was a long time since they had owned a dog. When Robbie left for Wales he took his sheepdog with him and they hadn't replaced him.

When James fell into a restless sleep she left, had a cup of tea and a scone in a café in the town and then went to the hospital, dreading the meeting with Chantelle.

She was right to be worried. Chantelle was impatient to be out, concerned about James and very aware that Katie was not as sympathetic to her partner as everyone else.

'How is he?' she asked. 'I need to get to see him.'

'He's sleeping more,' said Katie, honestly. 'He didn't recognise me. I think he's weaker, Chantelle.'

'He would be, now everyone he cares about has left him. I'm not stopping here another night. I should be with him.'

Katie didn't argue. 'I'll see if I can find a doctor,' she said.

It wasn't easy, she had to manoeuvre between people lying on trolleys in the corridor before she found someone who looked as if they were in charge. She waited until they turned from one patient to another and then said, 'Please, doctor, could Miss Cooper have a word? She wants to vacate her bed.'

It was the only message that could have got through to the harassed medic.

'Miss Cooper? The stabbing? Yes, I don't see why not. I'll be there in half an hour.'

Katie raced back to Chantelle. 'The doctor's coming. I think he's going to discharge you.'

'Tell the nurse. I need my things.'

'Hold on, he's not here yet. We need to prepare Rose. By then the shop may have closed.'

'Oh dear. Two of us will have to share a bed.'

'At least it's King size. I don't mind going in with Mum. Besides, if you're fit enough to visit James I shan't stay. Rose might want to – she's free for the next few weeks, but I should get back.'

It was late evening by the time Chantelle had seen the doctor, collected her medication and was ready to be discharged. Katie drove her back to the store and helped her up the steps to the flat.

'Don't fuss,' she snapped. 'I can walk perfectly well.'

Rose opened the door with a welcoming smile. 'I think I've found everything,' she said. 'I didn't know if you wanted supper so I waited.'

'I'd really like some bread and honey,' replied Chantelle, 'and a mug of cocoa, please, if there's enough milk.'

'What a great idea -super supper. You sit where you're comfortable and I'll get it. Come with me, Katie?'

Katie put down the bag of Chantelle's things that she had been carrying and followed her mother into the kitchen.

'Now, how was James?' asked Rose.

'Not well at all,' said Katie. 'I'm afraid he's ill – and not just with dementia. I'm sorry, I must go home in the morning.'

* * *

James hung on for another week but he seemed to have no fight left in him. In spite of being given antibiotics his condition worsened and he died of pneumonia the following Friday.

Chantelle was in pieces and Rose had to force her to help with arrangements for the funeral. James was to be buried in a woodland setting, like Rose's husband, 'Another one who preferred nature to religion' she grumbled.

She was also annoyed that she hadn't been in Sussex when Robbie departed for Australia. Katie would have to bring Bernard back for the funeral.

Heather insisted on coming and, as it was half term, Ryan was free to bring her.

It was a cold, grey day when the wicker coffin was lowered into the ground and Chantelle sang one of James's favourite songs to say farewell.

'I'll fly away' was more of a gospel song than the usual folk songs and it seemed appropriate to everyone, even Rose, although it did bring tears to her eyes and Heather was clinging to Ryan as if she was about to collapse.

A room in a local pub had been booked for the wake but, although they were all glad to be together, it was difficult to lift the feeling of gloom. With Chantelle's burglars still not caught there was an air of unfinished business and Chantelle herself seemed full, not only with sorrow but also anger at the hand fate had dealt her.

Once Katie had taken Bernard home and Heather and Ryan had gone back to Co. Durham, Rose had a suggestion for Chantelle.

'I have booked a holiday after Easter,' she said. 'It's a coach tour from Sussex to Cornwall. I've paid for it, and I didn't want to cancel but I don't want to leave you on your own. Do you think the boss would give us both time off together?'

'If it was after the schools go back, he might,' replied Chantelle. 'But where would I go?'

'That's easy. Why don't you come back to Sussex with me and stay with Katie for a week? I'm sure it would do you good.'

'I must admit I do miss the seaside – but what if all their rooms are let?'

'That's what we need to find out. I'd be quite content going away if I knew you were there with them, and we can come back together, ready for the summer season.'

'As long as he keeps our jobs open. I know I could do with getting away for a while. Thanks, Rose. I'll ask him.'

The warehouse manager agreed to let them both go.

'He likes having you here, Rose,' said Chantelle. 'and I don't mind doing the till. I was terrified he wouldn't employ me with only one hand.'

'He trusts you,' said Rose. 'I think he feels guilty he didn't have better security.'

'Well, we have now, and the police said some items have shown up on eBay. It might all be solved soon.'

'I do hope so.'

SIX

Heather sniffed the air as Ryan unlocked the door of their home in Seaton Carew.

'Your mother's been,' she announced. 'The place stinks of disinfectant.'

Ryan's mother, Lisa, lived near enough in Durham to pop in for frequent visits, but, although Heather liked her as a person, she could not get used to the way Lisa swept into the house and began tidying up and cleaning, as if the place belonged to her.

'I know she's only trying to help,' said Heather, 'but doesn't she realise how I feel?'

'It always looks great when she leaves,' he replied.

'But I'm not like that. I like things where I can see them, not all put away in a cupboard. I do clean, but not every room, every day. She makes me feel inadequate.'

'I'm sorry, love – but she's not here now. Let's get unpacked.'

Heather looked at the large vase of chrysanthemums in the centre of the dining table. It was very welcoming, she supposed.

'I thought going into politics, even if it was only local, would keep her busy,' she said, 'but she still wants to be part of your life.'

'It's understandable. She thought she'd lost me when I came back from Afghanistan.'

'Then she criticised me for going private. I could never have spent these few weeks going backwards and forwards to Kendal if I'd been working in the NHS.'

'She's a Socialist.'

'But doesn't she realise that by getting those who can afford it to pay for physiotherapy there's more time for the others to be seen at the hospital?'

'It's not worth trying to argue with her. Her heart's in the right place.'

'I know, if it hadn't been for her meeting Mum on holiday I would never have known you.'

How is it, she thought, that Blackpool had seemed to feature so strongly in their lives?

It was Blackpool that had reunited her with her grandfather, resulting in his move to Sussex to be near her, until he ran away with Chantelle.

Meanwhile Katie kept in touch with Lisa and John, Ryan's parents, and she shared their distress when Ryan, who had joined the army, was injured in Afghanistan and returned to a hospital in Liverpool where his leg was amputated.

It was there that Ryan and Heather met again.

Heather, a promising athlete, had been forced to

give up hurdling and, instead, had opted to become a physiotherapist.

While she was working in the hospital Ryan had come to her for rehabilitation and they realised they were meant to be together.

Invalided out of the army, Ryan had trained to be a schoolteacher and the pair set up home near his family in the North East.

Now Blackpool had featured again in their lives, with Heather's grandmother taking a holiday there.

'We've got a lot to thank Blackpool for,' Ryan laughed, and gave her a firm hug.

'I love you, Heather.'

'What, still? Fat old me?' she responded, her mood lightening. 'Let's see what's in the fridge.'

Lisa had only left a carton of milk and a bunch of grapes so they had tomato soup, crackers and cheese. 'I don't feel like tea,' said Heather, 'Let's have milky coffee. I don't think it will keep me awake tonight.'

'I'll make it' said Ryan,'You put your feet up.'

So she did.

Easter was very busy at the shop and the two women soon settled into a routine.

Rose found she could work well in the mornings but needed a break in the afternoons. Luckily there were students who were happy to work at weekends and, along with the two young male assistants, they covered the hours.

When the final week of April came Rose and Chantelle packed their bags and took the train south.

Katie was at the station to meet them.

'How was the journey?' she asked as she loaded their cases into the car.

'Slow,' said Chantelle. 'Your mother slept most of the way.'

'Well, I finished my novel,' said Rose, 'and I didn't feel like crosswords.'

'You'll need a magazine for the coach tomorrow,' said Katie. 'I've bought a couple. I hope you like them.'

'You are a good girl,' said Rose. 'It's a long way with nothing to do.'

She was worried. She hadn't had time to mentally prepare herself for another adventure. She really wanted a rest, somewhere peaceful and was afraid she might be forced to be sociable when she'd rather be alone. Still, she'd promised Bernard she would take lots of photographs, and it would be nice to be waited on instead of doing cooking and housework as well as being a saleswoman as she had been in the Lake District.

It was a joy to see Chantelle looking happier. She could go on holiday knowing that would work, anyway.

Rose couldn't fit in a hairdo this time. She would have to wait until she got to Cornwall.

Major Trent had said he wouldn't be arriving until mid week so she had time, even if it meant missing an organised trip. There were really only two trips that she was excited about- the day trip to the Eden Project and the morning to be spent at Port Isaac, the village setting for a television series with a grumpy doctor.

Once again it was with trepidation that she waited, in a window seat this time, to see who would be her travelling companion.

When the coach driver gave out the detailed itinerary Rose was pleased to see there was a free day on the Tuesday. As Major Trent was arriving that day this was the perfect time for her to have her hair styled.

She also intended to take the Saturday off as she felt she needed an extra day to explore on her own. Sunday was the day for the Eden Project, so the Major would miss it and Wednesday was the day for Port Isaac with a free afternoon for shopping for presents to take home.

At first she thought the seat next to her was going to remain empty but the coach stopped a little way along the coast and picked up three more passengers. The elderly couple moved to the rear of the coach and a thin, middle-aged man with a selection of bags stopped by her seat and loaded some of them onto the luggage rack.

He sat down with a slim case on his lap, unzipped it to reveal a small laptop computer and proceeded to scroll through the images on it.

Rose wriggled further into her seat and pressed her knees together to give him more room.

He noticed, looked up, and gave her a smile but said nothing.

Ah, well, thought Rose, at least I won't have to play games all the way with this one.

After a while she began to feel lonely. The couple behind her were chatting with a lady and her daughter across the aisle. The pair in front of her were reminiscing about holidays they had previously enjoyed and she was sitting in silence next to someone who only seemed interested in his laptop.

She tried to see what it was that occupied him but it was mostly pictures and each one did not stay on the screen long enough for her to study it.

She felt the need to disturb him to use the toilet and nudged him gently.

'Excuse me,' she said. 'Could you let me out for a moment?'

'Of course,' he replied and closed the lid of the computer immediately.

'I'm sorry if I interrupted your work,' she said as she returned.

'No problem,' he replied as he stood to let her back in.

'You're an artist?' she asked as she sat down.

'Oh no, just a photographer. I've been invited to supply some photos of seascapes and I thought Cornwall would be the best place to try to get something a bit different.'

'Are they all your photos?' she asked, pointing at the computer.

'Yes, I'm afraid so. There's only one in a hundred that's really special. I reject all the others.'

'Where do you take them?'

'Everywhere. I like photographing buildings and landscapes. Would you like to see some?'

'Yes, please. Have you any of Sussex?'

'Sure.' He scrolled through the images and paused at one of a windmill.

'Here, do you know where this is?'

'Oh, yes. Jack and Jill, on the Downs.'

'And this?'

'Brighton Pier, the old one – that's very atmospheric.'

'Taken at sunset,' he said, and proceeded to show her a collection of pictures of places until they pulled into a service station for lunch.

After lunch Rose took out her magazine. She felt she had taken up enough of the photographer's time. He had been kind enough to sit with her and introduce himself over lunch.

'Daniel Curtis,' he said.

'Rose Smith,' she responded. 'Pleased to meet you, Daniel.'

'You aren't eating much, Rose,' he said, looking at her coffee and muffin.

'My daughter made me some sandwiches,' she replied, 'but I didn't want to eat them in front of you on the coach.'

'No problem,' he laughed, tucking into a cheese and ham baguette. 'I'll bring my fruit slice with me and we can eat together.'

Rose relaxed. Her companion seemed friendly without being overbearing. She began to feel she might enjoy the journey after all.

Katie had packed ham and tomato sandwiches and a box of apple juice and her favourite cheesy biscuits. Although there was no smoking in the coach, passengers were allowed to take refreshments. In fact, the coach had tea and coffee facilities with crisps and nuts for sale.

Daniel packed his computer away and they ate their picnic as the coach drove through Devon and Dorset.

Rose was beginning to feel tired and, after putting away her empty box, sat back and closed her eyes. She was still asleep when they made their next stop.

'I must have a cup of tea,' she told Daniel as they exited the coach.

'Good idea,' he replied. 'You find a seat and I'll get them. Would you like a doughnut?'

'No thanks. I want to leave room for dinner,' she answered.

'I think I'll get a chocolate bar,' he said and joined the queue at the counter.

Rose blinked away the sleepy feeling she still had. The sun had gone in and the view of a busy car park outside did not appear enticing.

I hope the hotel is warm and welcoming, she thought, as she remembered Major Trent. She almost wished she wasn't going to meet him again. Pull yourself together, girl – it was all right last time. She supposed it was because her new friend had seemed so natural and casual, whereas Major Trent made her feel she had to try to impress him. Still – she would have three days to spend as she wished before the Major arrived. She climbed back into the coach, eager to arrive at their destination.

* * *

Heather looked round the kitchen of their little terraced house with pride. It might be on the edge of a Council estate but it had been allotted to them because Ryan was a key worker. It was new enough to be neatly decorated with plenty of cupboard space.

Were they ready? she wondered.

It was six weeks to the birth of their first child and now they were sitting at the breakfast table discussing names.

'If it's a boy I'd like him to be called Peter,' she said. 'Peter Walsh sounds good.'

'Hmm – too many boys would make fun of him,' replied Ryan, 'Pee – go to the toilet!'

'So that's why it's unusual these days. Kids can be so cruel.'

'How about Karen for a girl?'

'That's lovely. I like that. Walsh is such a short name we need at least two syllables. I know, your father is John, isn't he? What about Jonathan?'

'That's got a good ring to it. Mind you, there's a Jonathan at my school and everyone calls him John.'

'Your mother will have an opinion.'

'I know, maybe we'll ask about middle names. She's offering to buy a cot. She's getting very excited.'

'Well. There's nothing else to get but the pram and the baby seat for the car. I was going to look for them Saturday. Can you come?'

' Yes. There's no Junior football on at present and Pat is going to take over the swimming coaching for the rest of the year. I have the whole weekend off.'

'I think I've seen what I want so it shouldn't take long. We could have lunch at the Wimpy.'

'Great. Are you feeling OK? Is there anything you need before I go?'

'Just a kiss. See you about five.'

He rose and gave her a lingering kiss. She sat back in her chair and waited until she heard the front door close.

She wanted to pop into the clinic to find out how they were doing without her. She felt she had stopped work too early. She was thoroughly bored at home. She felt heavy and unfit. The sooner this baby came, the better.

Rose entered the dining room at the hotel to find all the tables set for four or six people. She was one of the first and sat with her back to the wall on one of the smaller tables.

She was pleased when Daniel came straight over to her and asked. 'Can I join you, Rose?'

'Of course,' she said. 'I hoped you would. I don't know anyone else.'

Gradually the room filled up and they were joined by an elderly couple. Rose tried not to stare but the husband had a full grey beard and she had to stop herself commenting on it. They introduced themselves as Mavis and Bert Stevens from Arundel.

There were only two choices on the menu and everyone on the table opted for the fish.

'It won't be like our chippie,' declared Bert.

'Hush, Bert,' said Mavis, 'Give the place a chance.'

It wasn't like usual fish and chips. It was cod mornay with sliced potatoes and peas. Rose consumed it with relish.

'No chips,' grumbled Bert and Mavis shot him an angry look.

Daniel was silent while he ate his meal and Rose felt obliged to continue conversing with Mavis.

'Have you been on many of these trips?' she asked.

'We do one every year,' replied Mavis.

'We're running out of places to go,' said Bert. 'Blessed woman won't go abroad.'

'There's plenty of places we haven't been,' said Mavis. 'I'd like to go to the lavender fields in East Anglia.'

'Not much there, too flat.'

'Where did you go last time?'

'Wales, Portmeirion,' said Mavis. 'It was charming.'

'Lots of fancy buildings, not much else,' said Bert, 'and the weather was crap.'

'Bert, language!'

'Well, I hope we get more sunshine this time – and the breakfast is better than this!' He finished his main course and frowned at the menu, 'They can't spoil apple crumble, I hope,' he said.

In fact, the apple crumble was lightly spiced and delicious, with smooth custard and a sprinkling of brown sugar.

'I wish I hadn't opted for ice cream,' said Daniel quietly to Rose.

Mavis and Bertie seemed engrossed in a discussion about coffee.

'I'd rather have tea,' said Mavis.

'Well, order it, then,' replied Bertie, 'and tomorrow we'll have some wine with dinner, if they have anything worth drinking.'

What a difficult man to live with, thought Rose as she excused herself and took the lift to her room. She could have spent the rest of the evening in the lounge but there was a folder in the room that explained all about the hotel, the meals, the fire escapes, local telephone numbers for emergencies and listed all the local sights. She would go to bed early and take that with her. Her eyes were heavy. It wouldn't take much to send her to sleep.

Saturday morning Rose was down early for her breakfast only to find that Daniel had already finished his and was about to leave the table.

'Morning, Rose,' he said. 'I'm just going to take some shots of the hotel before the trip. Are you coming,today?'

'No. I thought I would have a day to myself and explore the village.'

'Well, I expect we'll meet up at dinner. I think there's some music afterwards.'

'As long as no-one expects me to dance,' she said. 'I hope you get some nice photos.'

'I should do, St Ives is known for the light. See you later,' and he was gone just as Mr and Mrs Stevens entered.

Rose braced herself for another bout of grumbling but it took so long for Bertie to help himself to the sausages, eggs, bacon, beans, tomatoes, mushrooms and hash browns that she had finished her cereal and toast, made her excuses to Mavis and walked purposefully out to the reception area before he had time to sit down.

Leafing through the booklets about the village she found a guide book with a map that showed her she was a good twenty minute walk from the sea, but very close to the local museum.

Returning to her room she decided to do the walk before she became too tired and leave the museum for the afternoon.

She knew she would enjoy the walk but the feeling of freedom, almost euphoria, surprised her. Just for once nobody was making demands, she didn't have to plan, she hadn't got to listen to anyone else or provide help and advice. This was her time, and it was wonderful.

It was even better when she reached the cliff top and saw the great expanse of sea with little waves glistening in the sunlight. On either side of her a well trodden path wound across the grass covered ground. A small car park sat next to a wooden shack with an ice cream sign outside.

She was ready for a coffee and, hopefully, a toasted teacake. She pushed open the door and walked in.

The interior of the café was decorated with old photographs, ships and fishermen, mines and miners. The wooden tables were covered in blue and white checked cloths and there was as air of warmth and the scent of bacon frying.

'Good morning,' said the small lady behind the counter. 'Sit where you like and I'll bring a menu. All the specials are on the blackboard,' and she gestured to the wall behind her.

Rose sat down gratefully. The walk had been steeper than she was used to in Sussex.

'I'd like a coffee and a toasted teacake, please,' she said.

'Any special coffee? Americano, Cappuccino, Latte, Hazelnut?'

'Just filter coffee with cold milk, please,' replied Rose.

'Are you here on holiday?'

'Yes, on a coach trip, but I wanted a day to myself.'

'Well, you're in a bit early for most folks. We should get some more customers near lunchtime,' and she bustled into the kitchen.

Rose looked at the seagulls wheeling in the sky. She'd meant to have lunch here but it was only eleven o'clock. She'd have to go back into the village. No matter, she hadn't got a timetable.

Her teacake was beautifully toasted and covered with butter, real butter, not the spread that Katie insisted on using. Looking at the menu she realised she was in cream tea country. Perhaps she could miss out on lunch and treat herself to a cream tea this afternoon. There was sure to be somewhere else that served that.

It was only when she came to pay that she found she had forgotten to bring her camera. Although Katie had tried to get her to have a smartphone she had refused, preferring her old mobile phone.

'A phone is for calls, nothing else,' she'd argued. 'I don't want to be bothered with all the other stuff. Keep it for the computer.' But her phone did not take pictures so she would have to rely on her memory, or come back another day.

The little museum was housed in a converted chapel and Rose felt immediately at home. It wasn't all that different from her part of Wales. Mines were mines- no matter whether they were tin, coal or gold. The exhibits were displayed sensitively with stories of individuals as well as tales of construction, discovery and collapse. There was large photograph of a wheelhouse silhouetted against a light grey sky with a single shaft of sunlight illuminating the metal on one side, giving the picture an almost religious feel. Daniel must see this, thought Rose. I bet he'd love to recreate that.

Her wander through the museum over, she headed for

a cosy looking tea room. It was quite full but she settled herself at a corner table and picked up the menu.

She was hungry but determined to have a cream tea although it was only three o'clock. The café also advertised that it posted cream all over the country so she decided to send some to the rest of the family.

The scones, when they came, were warm and almost as large as the saucer under her cup. She had a shiny brown teapot and a jug of milk to herself, with a dish of butter as well as the jam and cream.

She devoured the first scone with relish, hardly noticing the hum of conversation around her but as she spooned the jam onto the second scone she suddenly felt sad. It was only a flash and she suppressed it – but she knew what had brought it on. This kind of experience should be shared. She had been content to be alone all day but suddenly she felt lonely.

SEVEN

Rose finished her tea and ordered the clotted cream for Katie and Heather and hurried back to the hotel.

Once in her room she took out the purple dress she had bought for Blackpool. It was the right outfit for a Saturday night but it didn't suit her mood. She had a grey midi skirt and a silver blouse that would do for this evening. There was only a light green trouser suit and the clothes she had chosen for the dinner with Major Trent that people hadn't yet seen her in.

When she entered the dining room she found many of the group had obviously come to dinner in the clothes they had been wearing all day. Daniel, however, was wearing a suit, without a tie, but with a broad grin on his face.

'Where are Mavis and Bertie?' she asked.

'They met up with another couple on the trip and found they had much more in common,' he said.

'But that's a bit inconvenient for the staff, tonight, isn't it, seeing that we pre-booked our meals?'

'Not really, our choices are all on little cards and they only had to move them to another table. Some people not with us left today so there's plenty of room.'

Rose looked down at the table. Each course had three choices but she and Daniel had both chosen roast chicken and crème brulee.

'I love treacle pudding but it could be a bit much after two courses,' he said, 'especially as I picked the soup.'

'I had to pick the lightest choices, too,' said Rose. 'That's why I went for the melon. I've already had a cream tea today.'

'Well done. Where did you go for that?'

'In the tea room next to the museum. You must go there, Daniel. There are some lovely photographs.'

'I will, on Tuesday. I got some great pictures today.'

'I forgot to take my camera – but I'll remember tomorrow.'

It was a relaxed meal and Rose went to bed in a happier, calmer state of mind.

Sunday morning she boarded the coach with the others and sat in the seat she had occupied before.

'Would you like the window seat?' she asked Daniel.

'No thanks. I sat there yesterday. You can enjoy the scenery today.'

Rose was wearing her light green trouser suit with a coral blouse. She secretly hoped Daniel would take a picture of her against a background of darker jungle plants.

When they reached the rim of the quarry Rose caught her breath. It looked to her as if the earth had been invaded by enormous transparent tortoises. Even the words, 'Eden Project' suggested something alien. They did not belong here, those domes, however fascinating they might be. However, they had been designed by man and she was hopeful she would feel different when she saw inside.

The Visitor Centre was almost enough to intimidate her with bright lights, a café and signs to the different domes.

'Let's get the land train,' suggested Daniel, 'Start from the other end and work back.'

'It looks as if it only goes half way,' said Rose, scrutinising the map that came with the guide book.

'Well, it's near the entrance to the biomes, anyway. That's where we need to be.'

She followed him to the train and on to the Rainforest Biome. He climbed up and along the walkway while she waited below, feeling uncomfortable in the heat and humidity.

Then they followed the Link to the Mediterranean Biome, with its olives, vines and citrus groves.

'Daniel?' she called out, 'Could you take a picture on my camera, please?'

'Of you? By the vegetation? Why didn't I think of that. Don't pose, look natural.'

She laughed and he snapped her then made her change position, sit and stand, until she pleaded with him to stop.

'Just one more for the album,' he said and took a picture of her with his own camera.

'I must have a cup of tea after all that,' she said. 'Right, café, here we come!'

By the time they had finished their meal of quiche and salad, which Daniel insisted should be completed with an ice cream, Rose was feeling overwhelmed.

It was all too much, too strange and too beautiful. She wished she had time to immerse herself in each area separately, to feel what it was like to live in those countries. It was like a trailer for the world and too much to take in in one day.

'I'm going to look in the shop and then find somewhere to sit down,' she said. 'You carry on if there's more to see.'

'OK, there's an outside garden and the Core, but that's full of kids. Where shall I meet you?'

'I'll be back at the coach at four o'clock,' she said. 'My head's buzzing.'

Luckily the shop was large enough for her to find a section near the plant sales where she could catch her breath and pretend to be searching for something to buy. In fact, she would have liked to purchase an orchid or a cactus but how could she get them home?

'Home' the word rattled around in her brain. Where was home? Was it the mobile home in Wales, Chantelle's flat or Katie's house – or should she look for somewhere else? She wanted somewhere she could end her days without worry, not too far from family, but not sharing with them. She still missed her cottage at Lane's End. 'Come on, old girl – look forward, not back,' she said to herself and went to choose some postcards, finding a nearby desk where she could sit and write them.

*　*　*

Monday's trip was to Truro. It was only a morning visit, to admire the cathedral and look round the shops. It began to rain on the way back and Rose was concerned. She knew her hair would curl up when it became wet and any style she had would be ruined. She and Daniel ran, together, from the coach to the hotel and were laughing when they entered, breathless. They decided to have a snack in the hotel bar and then retire to the lounge with newspapers and a book.

Daniel apologised for not accompanying her the next day.

'I'm off looking for dramatic views,' he said. 'So far it's been very predictable.'

'Don't forget the museum,' she said.

'I won't. See you at dinner.'

'Oh dear, I forgot. I think I may be joined by someone else.'

'A secret admirer?'

'No, silly. Actually, it's the owner of the hotel. Don't tell anyone, but I met him in Blackpool.'

'Well, if you want me to make myself scarce, just let me know.'

'This is very embarrassing. I don't even know if he'll be at dinner. I just know he's arriving tomorrow.'

'Don't fret about it. Let's wait and see.'

It was a good job they hadn't made arrangements as, when Rose, her hair styled and her grey skirt paired with a white blouse, entered the dining room that evening she found Daniel sitting at their usual table opposite Major Trent and a lady in a severe navy suit.

As Rose joined them the two men stood.

'Ah, Rose,' said Major Trent. 'So nice to see you again. Mr Curtis has been telling us what good company you have been.'

Rose blushed and took her seat next to Daniel.

'Rose, meet Celia – my sister. Celia, this is Rose Smith, the lady I have been telling you about.'

'Celia Stone,' said the lady, holding out her hand to shake Rose's. 'I hear you met my brother in Blackpool?'

'Yes,' replied Rose, completely nonplussed by the situation.

'And how is the hotel?' asked Major Trent.

'Lovely, perfect,' she stuttered. 'The perfect location' and she turned to Daniel for support.

'I've taken some pictures of the hotel and the garden,' he said. 'If you'd like to see them I'd be glad to show you.'

'We can always do with up to date photos for advertising,' said Celia. 'There's so much competition on line.'

They were interrupted by the waiter asking for their order and Rose buried her head in the menu. She'd taken so much care and invested so much nervous energy in this meeting and now it seemed the Major hardly noticed her. She didn't follow the rest of the conversation over dinner. She was just longing for it to end.

'My sister lives in the hotel in Malta,' she heard Major Trent say. 'She's only here for one night.'

'I have a conference in London,' Celia explained, 'and I took the opportunity to come over with Henry.'

She refused coffee and strode out of the room with just a nod.

'I'll just go and get those photos, then, shall I?' said Daniel.

'Please do – and if Rose and I take our coffees into the lounge we can look at them together,' replied the Major.

'Now, tell me what you have been up to since we last met,' he began, once they were seated.

'Nothing as exciting as going to Malta, Major,' she said.

'Henry,' he commanded. 'I think we know each other well enough for you to call me Henry, don't you?'

'It's funny. I just think of you as the Major.'

'So you do think of me?'

Rose blushed. 'Well.' She tried to retrieve the situation, 'I have been looking forward to this trip.'

'And Mr Curtis has been keeping you company?'

'Only at dinner,' she said, defensively.

'I must ask him if I can have you to myself Wednesday night. After all, it is a long standing arrangement.'

Rose was saved from replying by Daniel who sat down on front of them and laid out a large file on the coffee table.

'Here you are, Major. These are the local ones.'

He turned to Rose. 'You were right about the museum, Rose. It's a little gem and I found the site of that terrific picture. I don't think I'll ever get one as good as that.'

The Major looked through the file and smiled at Daniel.

'Could I purchase one or two of these from you, for exclusive use of the hotel?' he enquired.

'I'd be honoured,' replied Daniel.

'I would credit you, of course.'

'I'm sure we could come to an arrangement.'

'I'll give you my card and if you are ever in Blackpool, or Malta, you'd be welcome to do the same for those.'

'Holidays of Distinction,' Daniel read out. 'I'll remember that.'

He stood up. 'If you'll excuse me Major, Rose, I have to make some calls,' and, taking his folder, he left them alone.

'What a bright young man,' said the Major, pointedly. 'Life is so visual these days. Everyone relies on pictures, not words. It wasn't like that when we were young.'

'I suppose not,' said Rose, feeling uncomfortable that he had hinted at the difference in their ages. What was he trying to do? Make her feel she was closer to him than Daniel? Was there a hint of jealousy? Surely not.

'And how is the family?' Major Trent enquired.

'Much as usual. After my son-in-law's father died his partner came down to Sussex with me and is staying with Katie. My granddaughter's baby is due in June and I'm going up to Cleveland to help.'

'My – you are getting around almost as much as I do,' he laughed.

'That's what I was going to ask you about.' she said. 'It doesn't suit me. I like going on these little holidays but I want somewhere to call home, somewhere where I can make friends and contribute. I loved it in Wales but it's too far from the family.'

'Which arm of the family do you want to be near?'

'Katie, I suppose – but not in a mobile home, this time.'

'Do you have to make the decision now?'

'Not really. A lot of it depends on Chantelle. We have been living together in a flat but I don't know how much longer that will last.'

'I hope wherever you settle you'll be able to visit us in Malta next year. I do want to show you our beautiful island.'

'That's not quite the same as a coach trip.'

'Indeed. Perhaps you would like to bring Chantelle with you. Everyone speaks English and the golden buildings and the historical sites are unique.'

'You make it sound idyllic.'

'You'd only have to organise the flights. Once you were there you would be my guests. Please say you'll come.'

'I'll think about it.'

'And you will join me for dinner tomorrow?'

'I've been looking forward to it.' She didn't add that it was with very mixed feelings. 'Goodnight Major.'

'Henry,' he responded. 'Goodnight, Rose,' and stood to watch her leave.

'I've looked up the hotel website,' said Daniel, sitting down next to her at breakfast. 'It's Riverbridge Properties. They seem legit. But although Celia Stone is listed as a director there's no mention of Major Trent, and Holidays of Distinction isn't listed at all.'

'Perhaps he's what's called a sleeping partner,' said Rose. 'He uses the different name because it sounds better. After all, the holidays could use the hotels. It makes sense.'

'He did seem a bit too good to be true to me.'

'Don't say that - after he offered to buy your photos.'

'I suppose I shouldn't look a gift horse in the mouth. He likes you. He told me you had a date tonight. It doesn't matter. I'm not eating here anyway.'

'Oh, Daniel – you didn't do that because of me?'

'No, I'm going up to the café on the cliff, to get some sunset shots. They stay open until dusk. It will mean an early dinner but as our trip tomorrow is only a morning one that won't be a problem.'

'The Major has invited me to Malta next year.'

'Are you going?'

'It depends. I'd like to go abroad and that seems the best place to start but there are other people to consider.'

'Well, consider that scrambled egg before it gets cold,' he joked.

'I'm going to miss these breakfasts,' she replied.

The trip to Port Isaac was as enjoyable as she had hoped. Her fellow passengers were lively and even began to sing along to the songs on the radio. Everyone seemed so friendly and jolly- so different from the start of the holiday.

The weather was unseasonably hot and the bay looked just as it did on the television – only spoilt by the number of parked cars.

Daniel scowled. 'It's a real chocolate box scene but it's ruined by all those vehicles. I'll have to think of something different.'

'Such as?'

'Peeping round corners, close-ups of flowers, that sort of thing.'

'You mean, like that window box?'

Rose pointed to a large window box full of geraniums, crimson, scarlet, coral and pink, with a cascade of decorative ivy draping down, contrasting with the whitewashed cottage wall.

'Exactly. You catch on fast, Rose.'

'I like that sort of picture. I'll just sit here and enjoy the view and let you explore, shall I?'

'Thanks. I'll be back at the coach in an hour,' and he trotted off up the steep hill.

As Rose stared at the sea she made a decision.

If Chantelle was prepared to leave the store she would consider moving back down south. Rose wanted to live wherever she was needed for the time being but she also wanted to be somewhere where family members could help her if she got too frail. She might only have ten years left and she didn't want to be too far from family when her time came. Meanwhile she would enjoy having Chantelle as a companion. They had worked well together in the Lake District but she had the feeling they could both be happy near the sea.

She felt positive and energised as she packed to go home. The holiday had done her good but she was ready to go back. There was only one hurdle to overcome, the dinner with Major Trent.

CHAPTER
EIGHT

Rose studied her reflection in the mirror. It was Wednesday evening and she had treated herself to a rose pink dress. It had capped sleeves and the wrap around style finished at the knee. She was wearing heeled shoes, for once, and had varnished her nails to match her dress. With a dab of perfume behind her ears and on her wrist there was nothing more she could do.

She giggled to herself. If Bernard could see me now he'd remember he once thought of me as the robin lady, she thought. She couldn't do anything more about her height but the dress did take the eye away from the curve of her stomach. It was smart enough to make her feel satisfied but not too special to be unsuitable for other occasions.

She waited until the last minute and then paused in the doorway of the dining room. She couldn't see the Major at first and then noticed a table set slightly apart from the group and her date for the evening gave her a wave.

'You're making an exhibition of me.' she chided.

'And why not? I couldn't bear to be among all the chattering. They won't notice. They know I'm not on the tour.'

'I guess so. I hope nobody asks me to explain.'

'Let Daniel do the explaining. Do sit down and get comfortable.'

Rose sat opposite him and picked up the menu. 'What do you recommend?' she asked.

'Beef and mushroom pie if you're hungry or the pasta if you're feeling adventurous.' His eyes twinkled. Why did everything he said seem suggestive?

'I'll have the pasta,' she said, 'but without a starter. The puddings look delicious.'

'There's a favourite of yours?'

'Yes, lemon meringue pie. I have a weakness for meringue.'

The wine waiter hovered by the table.

'I'll have a bottle of Pinotage, please,' said the Major, 'and a jug of water.'

'Is that a red wine?' asked Rose.

'Yes, a gentle South African – not sharp. It will go with our first course but probably not with dessert.'

'You are having....?'

'The pie. I happen to know the chef does it with superb chunky chips.'

Rose looked at his smiling face and began to relax. What had she been so concerned about? He hadn't gushed over her. He just seemed ready to enjoy himself. It could be a pleasant evening after all.

By the end of the meal she felt both replete and entertained. Major Trent had been full of stories, many of them about the roads and buses in Malta or the strange complaints he'd had to deal with as a hotel owner.

'Someone complained of a ghost which turned out to be a branch hitting the window at night. We had to chop off half a tree.'

'Did it work?'

'The tree looked a bit lopsided but the customer seemed satisfied. How was your lemon meringue pie?' he added, spearing the last piece of blue cheese on his plate.

'Delicious,' she replied. 'I couldn't eat another thing.'

'How about a coffee? I'll ask them to bring it into the lounge.'

'Maybe I should. I feel a bit fuzzy.'

'Well, you look exquisite. You have real style, Rose.'

'You should have seen me plodding through our orchard in my wellingtons,' she giggled.

'I wish I had,' he said. 'I wish I'd met you years ago.'

Rose felt a shiver go down her spine. It was lovely to hear someone say that but it was too late, much too late to consider being more that a friend to another man. It wasn't as if her husband had set a very good example. She'd never really been complimented or cosseted. She didn't know how to respond.

'Is Celia your only sister?' she asked.

'Celia? Oh yes, one like her is enough. She's a real workaholic – but we won't see much of her when you come over to Malta. She's usually holed up in her office.'

'But you keep an eye on all your properties?'

'Yes, it's a good system- although we do have plans for expansion.'

'Another hotel?'

'Yes, in Italy. I'm going to investigate possibilities this autumn.'

'So we could both be house hunting?'

'You must let me see some of your options and I'll show you mine. You have an email address?'

'Yes, but I've hardly used it. It will be strange getting emails instead of letters and phone calls. I'm going to have to get used to Skype now Robbie is in Australia.'

She drained her coffee and tried to stand up but found she was wobbling on her high heels. Major Trent sprang to his feet and clutched her arm.

'Whoops!' he said. 'I think maybe I should escort you to your room.'

'It's all that red wine,' she said. 'I drank it too quick. I hope I don't have a hangover in the morning,'

'What time does the coach leave?'

'Nine o'clock.'

'I'll be there to see you off. Now, have you got your key?'

She felt in her bag and retrieved the key.

'Come along then, steady as she goes,' and holding her by the arm, he ushered her into the corridor.

By the time they reached her room Rose was adamant that she would never touch red wine again.

Major Trent opened the door and hesitated in the doorway.

'Are you all right from here, Rose?' he asked, with a tenderness she hadn't expected.

'I'm fine. Thanks, Henry,' she said. 'It was a lovely evening.'

He bent down and gave her a kiss on the cheek. 'I haven't had such a pleasant evening for a long time,' he said and squeezed her hand, hovering in the doorway as she made her way to the bed and sat down.

'You don't need anything?'

'No. I'm OK, now. Goodnight, Henry.'

'Goodnight, sweet Rose,' he said as he turned away and closed the door behind him.

Rose put her hands to her head and tried to focus. Had she ruined the whole evening? She didn't feel in control of herself. She'd have a drink of water and get ready for bed. He hadn't wanted to come in, had he? She wasn't ready to play games at her age, although it might have been nice to have a cuddle. How did one judge what a man wanted these days? It was just too complicated. She'd think about it in the morning.

There was a single rose by her plate when she went in for breakfast.

'I think Major Trent left it,' said Daniel. 'He's really sweet on you, isn't he?'

'Goodness only knows,' said Rose, dismissively. 'I haven't got anything for him. I feel stupid now.'

'You gave him your time,' said Daniel. 'I think he appreciated it. I've got something for you, too. Don't worry, it's nothing special,' and he handed her a brown envelope.

Rose took it and opened it gingerly. It was the picture Daniel had taken of her at the Eden Project.

The pale green of her suit looked perfect against the darker green of the vegetation and she had an enigmatic smile on her face.

' It looks as if I'm just going to laugh,' she said.

'You were, you were happy. I'm sorry I didn't have time to get it framed.'

'It's lovely – oh, I must take one of you before we go. I'll have a quick breakfast and we can use the hotel as a backdrop.'

She helped herself to cereal and a banana and shared his pot of tea.

Cases were being brought down and Daniel offered to fetch hers. Then he leaned on the door frame for her to take the photo and they exchanged numbers.

'Please sit in the same seats,' said the driver. 'I need to check that everyone is here.'

'There's the Major,' whispered Daniel as he stood at the bottom of the steps.

Rose turned back. 'I think I have you to thank for my rose,' she said.

'And I have you to thank for your company, ' said Major Trent, 'You will keep in touch, won't you? I'll be here for the next couple of months.'

'I will. I'll bore you with all the news about the baby,' she said, 'and thank you.'

It seemed natural, then, to move into his arms for a farewell hug. His lips brushed her forehead and she thought she heard him sigh.

There was a smattering of applause from the coach and she blushed in embarrassment. Eyes on the floor, she mounted the steps and crept to her seat.

'That wasn't necessary,' she muttered to Daniel.

'It wasn't me. People were just happy to see so much genuine affection.'

Is that what it was? she thought and lifted her head in time to wave goodbye to Major Trent and his Cornish hotel.

'What did you tell everyone?' she asked Daniel.

'They'd seen you two at dinner, so of course they were curious,' he replied. 'I just said he was an old friend. I didn't know they'd applaud.'

'I don't like being the centre of attention.'

'Well, you aren't any more. It was just a fleeting moment.'

'I hope nobody took a photo.'

'I don't think they were geared up for that – too busy getting settled. Anyway, what does it matter?'

'It matters to me.'

She slept most of the way home and just roused herself enough to bid farewell to Daniel. ' I can phone or email,' he said. 'I'll let you know when I'm having an exhibition.'

Somehow the light had gone out of her holiday. She was feeling more depressed the nearer they got to her stop. What would she find there? she wondered.

Had Chantelle enjoyed her week?

She need not have worried. Chantelle was bursting with delight when Rose arrived back at the Meadows.

'I met up with a couple of girls I used to know when I lived here,' she said. 'One's a divorcee and the other's a widow and you'll never guess what we've been doing!'

'Surprise me,' said Rose.

'Line dancing. They go twice a week and it's really fun and I can do it with one arm. I'm getting all the gear, the hat, everything.'

'What about the shop? Aren't you going back?'

'We've been talking about that. I was just waiting for you to come home. I think I would like to move back down here.'

'You would? Oh, Chantelle, that would be wonderful. It's what I was hoping you'd say.'

'But we couldn't both live with Katie.'

'I know – but if I sell the mobile home we could buy something between us, couldn't we? How much could you put down?'

'I'd need to check. The stuff James left is pretty valuable. It's finding the right buyers. It might take some time.'

'I'm coming back with you on Monday – then I'm waiting to hear from Heather. I won't be able to think about moving until September. You'll need to warn the shop but if we can find something by Christmas it would be perfect.'

'Hang on, you two,' chimed Katie. 'It takes months to buy a property and I doubt if there's anything down here that you would think suitable.'

'Nothing we could agree on, you mean,' said Chantelle.

'Think. Only one of you is a pensioner so you won't get special accommodation and if you want to buy no-one will give you a mortgage at your ages.'

'We might not need a mortgage,' said Rose. 'We need to talk to James's solicitor. That's a job for you when we get back, Chantelle.'

'I won't give my notice in until we are sure,' said Chantelle. 'I'd like to go on working when we get down here. Are there any vacancies at Bernard's garden centre, Katie?'

'Not that I know of, but, one step at a time. You can go on line and see what local estate agents have. I think you'll get a shock at the prices.'

Rose had two days to try to get used to the computer.

'Bernard? Can you supervise me while I try out my email?' she asked after supper.

'OK, Nan. What's your address?'

She took out a little notebook in which she had written instructions and passwords.

'Nan! You are supposed to remember your passwords, not write them down,' he said.

'Not at my age, darling. It's bad enough trying to remember a pin number for the bank.'

Bernard opened her email and she found two welcome messages, the first from Major Trent.

'I hope you got home safely,' it read. 'Best Wishes to all your family.'

'Who's that, Nan?' asked Bernard.

'Someone I met on holiday. How do I reply?'

He showed her and she pondered her response. Eventually, with two fingers, she typed, 'Good journey. Family well. Rose.'

She was sweating when she finished. 'That's really scary,' she said. 'I was afraid I'd do something wrong.'

'Well, press 'Send' and it will go,' said Bernard, 'and if you need to see if it has gone, look, there's a place that says 'sent.'

'I really will need someone watching me for a while,'

she said. 'I hope Chantelle feels more at home with it than I do.'

'Take it up to Heather's. Ryan will soon get you used to it,' said Katie as she came up behind them. 'I'm doing Chantelle a cocoa, Mum – want one?'

' Yes, please, that's something I didn't get on holiday.'

It's what I have been missing, she thought, family traditions.

Rose was surprised to find that once she was back in the flat her mood lifted and life settled back into its regular rhythm. She and Chantelle seemed to have achieved a sense of balance that suited them both. They each had their own tasks, Rose did anything that needed two hands and Chantelle did all the more cerebral tasks.

'I don't mind you reading my emails,' said Rose. 'There's nothing private and it might help me to remember.'

'There's nothing wrong with your memory,' replied Chantelle. 'You're just a coward when it comes to the computer.'

She was right. Rose was still afraid she might press the wrong button and everything she was writing would vanish.

'You ought to take lessons,' said Chantelle.

'Maybe, when we get back to Sussex.'

'Well. I've got good news for you. Heather has had her baby.'

'Why didn't she ring me?'

'I don't know. Katie sent the email. Perhaps Ryan is too busy.'

'What is it?'

'It's a girl. I don't know the weight. Why don't you ring Katie and find out more?'

So she did, but Katie couldn't help.

'I think it was a difficult birth,' she said. 'Heather is still in hospital. Ryan only sent a couple of lines.'

'Should we ring?'

'I don't think there'll be anyone at home and mobiles aren't encouraged in the hospital. It's better if we wait. I hope everything's all right.'

'Oh, Katie. It should be such a happy time.'

'I know, but don't panic.'

'I'll get packed. Please let me know if you hear any more.'

Three days later Rose had a call from Ryan.

'Hi, Rose,' he said. 'Sorry I didn't ring before but I was in the hospital. The baby is OK now. We had a bit of a scare. They kept them both in for observation but they came home yesterday. My mum is here, but, to tell you the truth, she and Heather don't get on. If I can tell her you'll take over next week is that OK?'

'Oh, Ryan. I've been out of my mind with worry. What have you called her?'

'The baby? Karen Louise.'

'And her weight?'

'Six pounds three ounces, but she was blue at first, Rose. We were so frightened.'

'How's Heather?'

'Still traumatised, I think. She seems incapable of thinking straight. She's tried to feed her but she's so tense. She's had to express milk. It's not what we expected, Rose.

I'm not sure what to do.'

'Are you working?'

'Kind of. They let me have some afternoons off. My mum's borne the brunt of it. The house is a bit of a battleground, to be honest.'

'You must have a district nurse or someone who comes round?'

'Yes, they try to help, but as soon as they've gone Mum and Heather are arguing again. It's not good for the baby. She sleeps for two hours and then she wakes up.'

'That's fairly normal at first. She'll settle.'

'Not if those two go on like this. Heather won't let Mum see to her in the night. It has to be her or me. I don't think she's getting much sleep at all and she seems angry with the baby. I'm sure Karen can sense it.'

The next call came from Ryan's mother, Lisa.

'Oh, Rose,' she said. 'I'm at my wits end. I've tried everything, but if I suggest something she does the opposite. I've tried helping with the baby but she gets so upset. It's 'the health visitor says this, the health visitor says that' and mumsnet is worse, and then when I try to leave her alone and get out of the way she ends up in tears saying she's a bad mum.'

'I've got my ticket for Monday,' replied Rose. 'I'm coming through Newcastle and should be there by three pm. Will Ryan still be in school?'

'Yes, but I've got my car. I'll meet you at the station. I do hope Heather calms down once you're here.'

'Let's just hope it's baby blues and won't last too long,' said Rose. 'Poor girl, she must be getting advice from so many places she doesn't know who to trust. I remember

I read Dr Spock but I didn't do everything he suggested.'

'Some people just have an instinct about these things,' said Lisa. 'I look forward to seeing you again, Rose. Katie has told me so much about you.'

'She told me about your new job at the Leisure Centre,' said Rose. 'Have they been OK about giving you time off?'

'I asked for compassionate leave,' she said. 'It wasn't easy, being nearly holiday time. I must be back for August.'

'Don't worry. I can stay as long as is necessary,' said Rose. 'I only volunteer in the store. Chantelle is the employee, but not for much longer, I hope.'

'She has plans?'

'We both have. I'll tell you about them when I see you.'

'Right. Karen's crying again. I'd better ring off.'

'Good luck, Lisa.'

CHAPTER
NINE

Chantelle was excited. It appeared that James had accumulated over sixty thousand pounds worth of jewellery as well as what he had hoarded in the flat.

'The only other bequest, as you know, is to Heather. It's a locket, with a picture of himself and a lady – his wife, I guess.'

'Bernard's mother, Anne,' said Chantelle. 'They parted when Bernard was about seven.'

'You want to sell it all and invest the money?' asked the solicitor.

'Rose and I are looking for a bungalow in Sussex,' she said, 'but the ones on line are about three hundred thousand pounds. I don't think she realises.'

'What will you do?'

'Try to get her to rent a flat. As long as I go on working we could afford that.'

'I wish you well. It's an expensive part of the country.'

* * *

Rose wheeled her suitcase out of West Hartlepool station. Lisa's car, big and sporty looking, was waiting in the car park and Lisa jumped out to help load Rose's luggage.

'Thanks, Lisa,' said Rose, 'I could have got a taxi.'

'My pleasure,' replied Lisa. 'I needed to get a few things, anyway.'

'You've done your shopping?'

'Oh, yes. It's straight back to the circus now.'

Rose was surprised to see Heather and Ryan's house was in a Close of quite modern semi detached homes.

'This looks nice,' she said, as they drove up to the open plan frontage.

'I bet you thought it was all back to back terraces,' laughed Lisa.

'Well, that's what we imagine when we visualise the North East.'

'These were all Council, but most of them have been sold to the residents. It's just a few, like Ryan's, that were kept for key workers. It's nice inside too, with three bedrooms and a good sized kitchen.'

Just then the door opened and Ryan came down the path to greet them.

'Hallo, Rose,' he said. 'I'll take that,' and he hugged her before wheeling her case into the hall.

'Do you need this or shall I put it upstairs?' he asked.

'Upstairs, please,' said Rose. 'I've got all I need now in my bag. Where's Heather?'

'I'm here, Nan,' came a voice from the kitchen. 'I'm just getting madam ready to see you.'

Rose paused at the door. Heather was holding the baby in one arm and trying to remove a bib with the other hand. Karen wriggled and the flap unfastened and the loose bib rubbed against her cheek.

She let out a wail and Rose watched her granddaughter's face flush with annoyance. She stiffened and the baby reacted by snivelling and waving her hands in the air.

'Let me have a cuddle,' Rose said, putting down her bag, shrugging off her coat, handing it to Ryan and holding out her arms to the baby.

'You're welcome,' snapped Heather. 'You wouldn't think she'd just been fed and changed, would you?'

'There, there, little one,' crooned Rose and the baby seemed to settle as she rocked her.

'I'll make some tea, shall I?' said Lisa.

'I'll do it,' said Heather, 'now Nan's got Karen. You lot go and sit down in the living room.'

Obediently they trooped into the next room and Ryan put a coffee table by the settee.

Rose's eyes lit up when she saw the rocking chair under the window.

'Is that yours. Ryan?' she asked.

'Yes, do you like it?'

'Very much. Could I sit in it?'

'With Karen? Of course. I often do that. She likes it.'

It wasn't long before the baby was asleep and Ryan showed Rose up to his bedroom where she put her in the basket by the bed.

'The next door room is really the nursery,' he told Rose, 'but Mum's in there at present. Will you be OK with that?'

'Is Lisa going home tonight, then?'

'She wanted to. She's left Dad on his own long enough. She said one extra body here was plenty. She didn't want to cramp your style.'

'I don't think I have a style,' said Rose. 'I just handle things as they come along.'

'Well, up until now I'd say you'd handled things very well. Heather used to be wonderful but now she seems so unsure of herself.'

'She'll get better,' soothed Rose. 'It's only temporary. Nobody gets trained for their first baby. You just learn on the job.'

When they returned downstairs Heather had brought in a tray of tea and biscuits. She sat stiffly on a dining chair looking as if she was waiting to be accused of something.

'I suppose Lisa's been reporting me to Mum,' she said at last.

Lisa put down her cup. 'It's only natural she'd want to know how you're coping,' she said.

'Or not coping,' said Heather.

'It gets easier with practice,' said Rose. 'Give yourself time.'

'It's probably easier without interference,' said Heather.

'Well, I won't be interfering any longer,' said Lisa, rising from her chair. 'Maybe when you are feeling better you'll let me know. Ryan? I think I know when I'm not wanted.'

'OK Mum, I'll get your things,' said Ryan and followed her upstairs.

'All right, all right,' grumbled Heather. 'I didn't realise what a Mummy's boy he was.'

Rose did not reply. Once Lisa had driven off she took the tea things into the kitchen.

'You'll have to show me where everything is and let me know your system,' she said.

'I wish I had a system. I just act on command,' said Heather. 'She commands and I act.'

'You mean the baby?'

'Of course. You didn't think I meant Lisa?'

'You do know you are in charge, don't you?'

'Me? That's a laugh. Everyone knows more about bringing up a baby than I do.'

'Why don't you go and lie down while she's asleep?'

'I'm allowed to do that?'

'Don't be sarcastic. What did you plan for Ryan's tea?'

'Ask him. I think he was going to get fish and chips.'

'Right, you go and get forty winks and he and I will organise something for later.'

'Great, Nan. I feel better already,'

Heather seemed to haul herself to her feet and trudge up the stairs and Rose went looking for Ryan. He was in the garden shed, pumping up the tyres on a bicycle.

'There's not much you can't do with a false leg – is there Ryan?' she said.

'No. I wouldn't like to trek to the north Pole on it,' he said, 'but I can drive, walk, dance, even.'

'What do the children at school think?'

'If they remember they are just curious. They love it when I get into the pool without it. I think it makes the weaker ones feel empowered.'

'Heather says you are getting fish and chips.'

'Yes, I thought we'd break you in gently. She hasn't been doing much cooking.'

'Well, with a bit of luck Karen will give us time to enjoy it.'

'I'll show you how we do her bottles and that should make things easier,' he said.

In fact, they had to wake Heather for supper. Baby Karen had been fed and changed and was lying in her pram in the living room when a bleary eyed Heather eventually came downstairs.

'Why didn't you wake me?' she asked.

'I was just showing Rose what to do,' said Ryan. 'It's not quite the same as over forty years ago.'

'That smells good. I'm starving. How have you kept her so quiet?'

'Just rocking the pram,' said Rose. 'And we put on some soothing music. You've got a great collection of CDs, Heather.'

'The computer says Mozart's best,' said Heather. 'We haven't any Mozart.'

'Anything with a steady rhythm, and the human voice is good, not always tinkling brooks and rushing tide.'

'Ha! That's very New Age, Nan.'

'Well, I'm Old Age,' laughed Rose. 'Now eat up. This fish is lovely.'

'I hear you've been gadding about the countryside, Rose,' said Ryan.

'Only Blackpool and Cornwall,' replied Rose. 'Just coach trips.'

'And Mum says you met someone,' said Heather.

'I met lots of people – a very nice photographer and a Major.'

'And one of them asked you out?'

'Asked me to go on holiday – to Malta.'

'Are you going?'

'I'm not sure. It depends on Chantelle,' and she told them about their plans to move south.

When Karen started grizzling again Rose watched Heather change her and give her a drink of water and then she suggested they take her out in the pram.

'It's a nice evening and it's still light. I'd love to see the sea,' she said.

'Right, we'll wrap the little one up warm and show you the sights,' said Ryan.

Walking along the front Rose hoped that she would be able to have the desired effect and help her granddaughter to adjust to the demands of motherhood.

It wasn't easy. Heather was woken again in the night and was in a bad mood in the morning.

'I can't do this,' she said to Rose. 'I just look at her and I think – you little tyrant. I don't feel like a person. I feel like a slave. When she won't stop crying I want to shake her. I frighten myself sometimes.'

'Don't feel it always has to be you. Use me. That's what I'm here for. We can share the difficulties.'

'I hated it when Lisa could settle her and I couldn't.'

'It isn't that you don't care enough – it's because you

care too much. You expect too much of yourself. Let me help. I won't be here for ever.'

'I read on line the doctor could give me pills.'

'Stop looking on line. Do what you feel is right. Every baby is different and so is every mother. Karen has to get used to you, talk to her, sing to her, talk rubbish if you like. Just make a connection.'

'No one else has put it like that. What do I do when she wriggles?'

'She either wants skin on skin or is uncomfortably hot or wet. If you aren't breast feeding do you cuddle her?'

'Not with no clothes on.'

'Try it, and breathe slowly, calm yourself down.'

'Nan, you're a genius.'

'Not really. I just believe in being as natural as possible. After all, we are animals.'

'I'd never thought of it like that.'

'Well, what shall we do today?'

'Let's take her to the park. I don't feel quite as lazy as I have been. Then, this afternoon, I'll show you how I bath her.'

'That should be fun.'

'Perhaps.'

Rose watched as Heather put a waterproof sheet down on the carpet. Then she half filled the baby's bath with warm water, brought in another jug and added it, tested it, ensured all the necessary nappies and creams were nearby and proceeded to undress Karen while sitting on the floor.

'Who suggested you do it like this?' enquired Rose, incredulous.

'No one. The bath had legs but I didn't trust them. This is the only time she seems happy. I like doing everything on the floor.'

'That's because you are so flexible,' said Rose. 'Most people would find it uncomfortable.'

'I'm not most people. Look, she loves it!'

And watching Karen, her head supported by her mother, kicking and waving her arms, Rose began to hope that everything would be all right.

'I'll do her bottle,' she murmured as she felt tears come to her eyes and she retreated to the kitchen.

Heather wrapped the baby in a towel and sat, cross legged on the floor, feeding her. For the first time since she had arrived Rose felt they looked content.

Heather was humming to herself and Karen snuggled against her mother's chest. Shyly, Heather lifted her T shirt and held the baby close to her.

'I'm sorry, sweetheart,' she murmured, 'I tried. I really did.'

Looking up at Rose she smiled weakly. 'I won't do this when anyone else is around, you realise.'

'You look beautiful together.'

'I still don't know what they mean by 'bonding.' I don't feel a connection. She's a separate person.'

'Don't worry about it. She's happy to be with you. That's all that matters.'

'Well, she is now. It doesn't last.'

'You know babies can pick up accents while they are in the womb?'

'Oh, Nan, don't be ridiculous.'

'I'm not. She knows your voice – so keep it calm,

even when she's upsetting you. You know 'Singing in the Rain'?'

'Of course.'

'Remember when Gene Kelly is on set in the silent movie scene?'

'He says I love you, I love you, I love you.'

'Yes, but not then. When he's angry with his co star and, because no-one is picking up the sound, he tells her how horrible she is while pretending to be billing and cooing.'

'Billing and cooing? Nan – get real!'

'You know what I mean, look loving, sound loving but say ' I think you are the most awkward unreasonable little horror I have ever met."

Heather burst out laughing and the startled baby released the teat and cried out in alarm.

'Now, look what you've done,' Heather giggled. 'Here, take her for a minute.'

Still laughing she handed the baby to Rose who held her over her shoulder for a burp. Then she sat in the rocking chair and, taking the bottle from Heather, offered it to Karen. At first she thought the child would refuse and start crying but she settled her on her lap and cooed gently to her. The final third of the bottle was soon finished and Karen's eyes were closing.

'That was the best afternoon I've had since I came home,' whispered Heather as she fastened the babygro and placed Karen in the pram.

'This really works as a cot,' muttered Rose. 'I like the way it comes to bits, not like the big one I had for your mother. I used to keep that in the porch.'

'Carry-cot, pushchair and baby seat – all in one, and everything folds down. It's the modern way, Nan.'

'I suppose it's better, but I did like seeing a row of white terry nappies blowing on the line.'

'You are funny, Nan. Surely that was a lot of work?'

'Not with my old twin tub. What happens to those nappies when you've finished with them?'

'I don't know. I suppose they're incinerated.'

'Mmm. I wonder.'

'Look it up on Google.'

'Don't ask me to use that blessed computer. Chantelle does all the looking up for me.'

'Well. I'll empty this bath and we can look up your friend's hotel in Malta. How about that?'

'We'll have a problem. I don't even know what it's called.'

'You know the name of the firm, don't you?'

'Riverbridge Properties.'

'So we look them up and see what they own.'

Sure enough Riverbridge Properties owned the two hotels Rose had visited and another in St Paul's Bay.

'It's called 'Harbourside,' said Heather, ' Managed by Celia Stone. Is that the one?'

'Yes. I met Celia. She's a bit cold.'

'Not like your friend the Major, then?'

'Don't tease, Heather. It's really not like that.'

But it was nice to be teased, nice to see Heather with a smile on her face. If this carried on she would be able to go back to Wales in August and organise the sale of her mobile home.

CHAPTER
TEN

The Evans family were quite happy to purchase the mobile home from her. The new shepherd was getting married and needed somewhere to live. She would have well over a hundred thousand pounds to put towards her next residence.

It had been a struggle, getting Heather to feel confident, but when she said to Rose, 'I'm sorry, Rose, I can't do that grumpy talk any more. I just want to tell her how cute she is and how much I love her,' Rose knew she had succeeded.

'I used to treat her as if she knew what she was doing,' said Heather. 'Now I realise life was just as confusing for her as it was for me. Poor little mite – she didn't mean to antagonise me.'

'That comes later,' said Rose. 'when she's about thirteen, or probably earlier, these days.'

'Mother and baby club is helping. Meeting all the

other mums going through the same thing makes me feel better. We've got a good little crowd, now. Four of us have arranged to meet up in town once a week.'

'And Ryan is off from next week so it's time I left,' said Rose. 'Once I've checked in with Chantelle I'm off to Wales. They always need help in the school holidays.'

'Thanks a bunch, Nan,' said Heather. 'We'll miss you.'

While Rose was in Wales Chantelle had a phone call from Katie.

'Chantelle, I don't know if you'll be interested but Bernard came back from a weekend away with the disabled group he helps at with some news. The charity he belongs to owns a shop with a flat above it. They are about to advertise for a new manager who could rent the flat. I don't know where in town it is, or any of the costs involved but I can give you their number.'

'Katie, that might suit us very well. It wasn't what Rose was looking for but it might be all we can afford. I'd love to manage a charity shop. I do hope they don't get a lot of interested people.'

'I don't think the pay is too great but you should have a good chance, with your experience, and Rose could volunteer like she does now.'

'She's selling her mobile home to the Evans's. That should go through in a few weeks. It feels like fate, Katie. Thank Bernard for me.'

She could hardly wait to tell Rose but how, and when? She'd have to find out more before she tried to convince her. There was so much that could go wrong. She mustn't get her hopes up.

Chantelle sat down to create a query letter, listing all the questions she should ask the charity. Then, with that in front of her, she rang the number that Katie had given her.

The person on the other end of the phone seemed surprised, at first, that she knew the situation.

'We haven't advertised, yet,' she said. 'How did you know?'

'My late partner's son is one of your volunteers,' she replied. 'Bernard. He knew I was looking to move south and, as I work in a shop, he thought I would be interested.'

'Bernard? Oh, yes. He's one of our best helpers. Would you like me to send you the details as soon as they are finalised? Have you an email address?'

'Yes, please. I would be very grateful. I could come for an interview. I could stay with Bernard.'

'Where are you now?'

'I'm in the Lake District - but I'm renting at the moment so there wouldn't need to be a long delay.'

'As you can imagine, we would like to re-open before Christmas. If you'll give me your contact details I'll get back to you.'

'Thank you,' said Chantelle and proceeded to comply.

Her next task was to update her CV and get some recent references. Guy Brown would give her a good reference but it would be useful if she had one from a charity. The only one she had any contact with was the RSPB. She had been on some bird watching treks with them and installed a collection box in the store.

Would that do, or would the Care Home be better?

She wished she'd been more involved with the church but she'd left that to Rose. She was impatient to tell her about the possibility of a job with a home but, instead, she rang Katie to warn her not to tell her mother until she knew more about it.

'I thought you'd say that,' said Katie. 'I do hope it works out. Think what a lovely Christmas we could have with us all here.'

The details arrived on the computer the next morning. Chantelle forced herself to wait until the shop closed before she printed them off and studied them carefully.

The charity shop wasn't in the centre of town but it was in a well used shopping parade on the outskirts. The flat above had its own entrance but, unfortunately, had only one bedroom.

The managerial position wasn't very well paid and the rent for the flat would eat into a large chunk of it. If that's how much a one bedroom flat would cost, she thought, a two bedroomed one would be much more. Rose would have her pension and the money from the sale of the mobile home, but would she be prepared to share a bedroom?

There were photographs of the shop, the downstairs storeroom, toilet and sink and the upstairs, with a new bathroom and kitchen and a large living room with a reasonably sized double bedroom. The flat had been freshly decorated with carpets in the living areas and matching vinyl in the hall and kitchen. Of course, there was no garden but it was within walking distance of the park and the beach. Better still, it was on a bus route to Katie's village.

Chantelle could hardly wait for Rose to return. As soon as the Bank holiday was over she confessed to Guy what she had been planning and explained her situation.

'I wasn't going to ask you until I had somewhere to go,' she said, 'but if I apply for this job I'll need a reference. The thing is, until I talk it over with Rose I don't even know if I should apply.'

'Go for it, Chantelle. It won't be a problem finding someone else for the shop if we have an empty flat for them.'

'Thanks, Guy. I will. I'll go to Wales and try to persuade Rose this is ideal for us.'

Rose was surprised to get a call from Chantelle asking if she could come and stay for a few days.

She's up to something, she thought, but it will be good for her. I hope she doesn't feel too cramped.

She was even more surprised when Chantelle showed her all the information about the charity shop.

'We need to decide soon,' she said. 'There may be other people interested.'

'What makes you think they'll choose us?'

'We can only try. It may be the only way we can afford to live down there.'

Rose was disappointed. She'd been dreaming of recreating the life she'd had on the Downs with Katie, Bernard and Heather. Of course, she wasn't fit enough to run a smallholding but was she ready to live in a flat over a shop?

'Silly me,' she told herself. 'That's what I've been doing for months.' But it wasn't quite the same. This would probably be her last home. She needed to go to Sussex.

Unfortunately Katie's house was full of paying guests so Rose and Chantelle booked into a B and B.

Chantelle had sent in her application and waited impatiently to hear from the charity. They had both walked past the empty shop and Rose agreed it was in a perfect position. The parade of shops had a hairdresser, a butcher and a newsagents' as well as a convenience store and a Post Office.

Then one morning, Rose found she had an email from Major Trent.

'I shall not be in Blackpool this autumn,' he wrote, 'I am in Italy and I believe I have found the perfect building for our next hotel. It's a castle in Tuscany. We have put down an initial deposit but buying property here is quite complicated so it may take some time. I hope to be back in the UK by Christmas. I hope all is well with you, love, Henry.'

'Oh dear,' she told Chantelle. 'I forgot I was going to email him about the baby. Still, I don't suppose he would have been interested.'

'He'll be more interested in the flat and the shop,' said Chantelle. 'Tell him about that.'

'You watch. See I do it right.'

'You only have to click on reply.'

'I need to think what to say, first.'

'No you don't, you can edit as you go along. I know, you dictate and I'll type.'

So she did, and once Rose was satisfied with the result they sent the message.

Katie was impatient to hear about Heather and arranged to meet them in the café on the pier.

'This is nice,' said Rose, 'being able to see the sea while we drink our coffee.'

'It's open during the intervals in when the shows are on,' said Katie.

'That reminds me,' said Rose. 'Heather and Ryan went to the cinema one evening while I was there. It was the first time they'd been out together for months. She was so happy.'

'What a relief. I was concerned when you told us she was suffering.'

'Ryan was very patient. Not all men would have understood.'

'She's a lucky girl.'

'I'm lucky, too,' chimed Chantelle. 'I had a call on my phone today. I've been invited for an interview at the charity's headquarters. It could mean we've got the shop.'

'Don't get too excited,' said Rose. 'There may be lots of others in the running.'

'Have you sold the mobile home, Mum?' asked Katie.

'More or less. I have put my stuff into storage. The Evans's have given me a fair price.'

'So you've burnt your boats, then?' said Chantelle.

'Not necessarily. I could always get another one,' she teased. 'There's plenty of sites around.'

'All off the beaten track,' said Katie. 'Don't think of it. I'd rather you stayed with us.'

'Well, we don't have to decide now.'

'And you don't have to stay in the B and B next week. I'll have one of the bedrooms free if you don't mind sharing.'

Rose laughed. 'We might have to get used to it,' she said.

Chantelle was nervous as she mounted the stairs to the charity's office.

The young woman at reception had been friendly and, through an open door, she had seen some kind of exercise class going on in a large hall. There was a notice board on one wall of the corridor with lists of events and activities.

'Mrs Dunn will see you in her office,' said the receptionist. 'It's just at the top of the stairs, or would you rather use the lift?'

'The stairs are fine,' replied Chantelle. 'Thank you.'

There did not appear to be anyone else waiting so Chantelle knocked gently on the door and was rewarded with a cheerful 'Come in.'

The lady who stood and came round the desk to greet her was large in every way. She towered over Chantelle, her large bosom competing with her broad hips to attract attention, both clothed in a shiny fabric dotted with colourful peonies.

Chantelle tried to concentrate on the woman's face – but was mesmerised by the hand that stretched out to greet her. It was covered in rings, two or three on each finger, all different colours and designs.

She shook it carefully and Mrs Dunn smiled.

'Do sit down, Miss Cooper. May I call you Chantelle?

It's such a pretty name.'

'Yes, please, Mrs Dunn,' replied Chantelle.

'You showed an interest in managing our shop. You have been in retail?'

'Yes.' Chantelle told Mrs Dunn about the shop she used to own in Stable Lane and the store in the Lake District where she and Rose Smith had worked together until the theft.

'You have a weak arm, I gather?'

'Yes, from the burglary. I was stabbed. I can move it but I have no feeling in my hand.'

'There's nothing that can be done?'

I could have a prosthetic arm, I suppose, but, with Rose's help I can do most things with one hand.'

'And you and Rose would wish to occupy the flat over the shop? Would that be a permanent arrangement?'

'As permanent as my employment,' she answered. 'We have nowhere else to live unless we stay with Bernard.'

'Ah, yes. Bernard. He speaks very highly of you.'

'I lived with his father until he died.'

'I see. If I take you to see the property and tell you all the financial details perhaps we could see if it suited you.'

'Now?'

'I don't see why not. Was there somewhere you had to be?'

'No, I'm sorry. I wasn't prepared.'

'I feel you are the right person for the shop but I expect you need to consult with your companion about the living arrangements. I won't expect a decision until then. We do have to ensure that anyone with a disability is given every opportunity.'

Chantelle relaxed. Now she understood why she had been interviewed. The fact that she had a useless arm had put her at the top of the list of candidates. Her disability had turned out to be an advantage. She could hardly believe her luck.

The flat was just as she had seen it on line, with a view over the rear gardens of the houses in the street behind. It was light and airy with plain painted walls, white woodwork, modern window blinds and a gleaming kitchen, with more cupboards than she could count.

'It's beautiful,' she gasped.

'But there's only one bedroom,' said Mrs Dunn.

'Yes. I need to let Rose see it,' said Chantelle. 'It's big. She might think it's OK.'

'I hope so. I'll let you have details of the rent and all other expenses. Your salary for managing the shop is set by the charity and you have responsibility for recruiting volunteers. You'll need at least two others besides Mrs Smith. As for stock, as you can see we have started with some from our other shops but we need to build it up with local contributions.'

They were standing in the shop and Chantelle was delighted at the wall of wooden shelves containing paperback books and the racks of clothing arranged in sizes.

'There's a steam iron provided and plenty of storage space through here,' said Mrs Dunn, 'and a back way to the yard outside with a fire escape from upstairs. The bins are collected from the service road behind the shops and there is room along there for one vehicle but I wouldn't advise it.'

'I'm afraid I don't drive,' said Chantelle.

'Of course. I was forgetting – and nor does Rose?'

'No. She gave up a few years ago.'

'Then you'll need a delivery driver. You can see there's plenty to do if we want to be open in November.'

'I'll bring Rose as soon as possible. When would be convenient?'

'This afternoon? About four?'

'Certainly. I can't believe she won't like it. It's perfect.'

'I'll get a contract drawn up. Can you live with Bernard until you move in?'

'I'm sure we can. We'll need time to furnish it. Thank you so much, Mrs Dunn.'

CHAPTER

ELEVEN

On the bus back to Katie's Chantelle began to feel apprehensive. Had she been too enthusiastic. Could they afford £500 a month between them? Would Rose refuse to sleep in the same room? Would her salary be enough to pay for electricity, food and living expenses?

They would need a television, two beds, a dining table and chairs and at least one sofa. The idea of choosing it all was thrilling but it depended on Rose.

She could hardly eat her lunch as she told Katie and Rose about the flat.

'Do you think Mrs Dunn would mind if I came, too?' asked Katie.

'I think that's a good idea,' said Rose. 'You might stop Chantelle making all the decisions.'

'I wouldn't,' said Chantelle. 'If you don't like it we don't take it.'

'Good – as long as that's settled.'

Rose was unusually silent as Mrs Dunn showed them the flat that afternoon. It was Katie who asked all the questions – about insurance and security.

Rose took a deep breath. The place had a fresh paint and new carpet smell but nothing unpleasant about it. The new windows were double glazed and the traffic at the front was reasonably light. There were no obvious noises or scents from the neighbouring properties. There were no signs of damp and the fire escape looked in good repair.

She tried to picture the bedroom with a fitted wardrobe, dressing table and two beds. It was at the front, with a large bay window. Next door was the bathroom and the L shaped lounge and kitchen were at the back of the building.

'You could change the rooms round?' suggested Mrs Dunn, 'especially if you like to eat in the kitchen.'

'It depends where I have my computer,' said Chantelle. 'That L shaped room could give me a little office corner.'

'What do you think, Mum?' asked Katie.

'It isn't what I expected,' said Rose, slowly, 'but it's got much more going for it than our flat in the Lake District. It's so fresh and clean. It would be like starting new.'

'And don't you want to?' asked Chantelle.

'Actually, Chantelle. I think I do,' said Rose with a grin. 'Mrs Dunn, I think you've found us a home.'

'Well, the sooner we start, the better,' said Mrs Dunn. 'If you come in on Monday morning, Chantelle, we'll make a list of everything we need for the shop and you can design an advert for volunteers. I can give you one lady from another shop to help get you started. We can begin to plan for an opening in October. Welcome, ladies. I wish you every success.'

'Can we order some furniture for upstairs before the shop opens?' asked Rose.

'Of course. The charity is paying for everything at present. We don't charge rent until you actually move in. Remember, some of our shops have good quality chairs and tables. You don't need to buy everything new.'

'No,' said Chantelle. 'Just new beds. Oh, Rose, this is so exciting.'

Looking at her friend's face Rose couldn't help feeling happy. She looked ten years younger, and she crossed her fingers that everything would work out fine. I just hope I can go on managing stairs, she thought, then I can stay here for ever.

On their return to the Meadows Rose sat down to compose an email to Major Trent.

There wasn't much on his business card. Just, 'H.O.Trent. Holidays with Distinction.' She wondered what the 'O' in his name stood for. There was a mobile telephone number and an email address : hotrent@ gmail. com. It made her smile every time she looked at it. He must have thought it a real joke to make it 'hot rent!'

She gave him the address of the shop and the charity and told him she would be sharing the rent of the flat with Chantelle, rather than looking for a freehold.

She still had a few pieces of jewellery left that the solicitor had not sold for her and she intended to change her bank details as soon as possible. Meanwhile, she would not splash out on everything new. She still had perfectly serviceable bedding and cutlery, pots and pans. As soon as she had the key to the flat she would send for her belongings in Wales.

She was looking forward to using the big double oven in the flat's kitchen. It wasn't easy to bend without pain and that would be a real treat.

'We'll need a fridge,' said Chantelle. 'The modern ones are more efficient.'

'Let me buy you one as a house warming present,' said Katie. 'We can go and look in the sales. You'd better have a fridge/ freezer.'

'Remember,' said Rose. 'We have to check out the charity shops for furniture.'

'I know,' said Chantelle. 'We'll do that on Saturday.'

By the second week of October the shop was full, Chantelle had recruited two volunteers, a man and a woman, and they were ready for the great opening.

The charity was providing drinks and nibbles and the mayor was going to cut the ribbon. It was a Tuesday morning and there was a small gathering outside the shop at 10.45 when the mayor arrived.

Katie noticed a reporter and cameraman from the local paper and a number of clients from the disabled group. The door, she noticed, had been made wide enough to allow a wheelchair to enter and there was no step.

Mrs Dunn was resplendent in a puce coat and hat and Chantelle looked very businesslike in a navy skirt and scarlet jumper.

A table had been set out at the front of the shop so that food and drink did not ruin the contents, but people wandered in and out and Rose was concerned that some of the clothes might get damaged.

'Don't worry, Rose.' whispered Chantelle. 'The best stuff is safe out the back.'

Terry, the volunteer, was on the till, wrapping and packing purchases for the customers, while Joyce stayed outside serving drinks, only hurrying back through the shop to replenish the jugs of Bucks Fizz.

By one o'clock the crowd had dispersed and they all sat down in the store room in relief.

Bernard was hovering in the shop doorway.

'Would you like me to fetch some hot dogs?' he asked.

'Oh, Bernard, what a good idea,' said Katie. 'Will that suit everyone?'

'I'd rather have a bacon bap,' said Terry.

'And me.' said Chantelle. 'And me,' said Rose.

'OK, bacon baps all round,' said Katie. 'I'll come with you, Ned.'

'I'll get the kettle on,' said Rose.

'How much did we take, Terry?' asked Chantelle.

'A few hundred. I haven't counted it properly yet. It's a good start.'

'Not every day will be like that, but you all did very well, thank you.'

By Christmas Rose and Chantelle had settled into their new lifestyle.

Chantelle had met up with her friends and went line dancing twice a week.

Rose had discovered the library and had begun to go out to the pensioners days at the cinema. Sleeping in the same room had not turned out to be a problem. Neither lady snored and each had their own chest of drawers and wardrobe. Rose enrolled in a cookery class at the local college and they worked together happily in the shop.

It was when she received a large Christmas card from Major Trent that Rose remembered that she had promised to visit him in Malta.

'He did say I should bring you, but we can't both leave the shop at the same time,' she said to Chantelle.

'He didn't really want me there. He was just being polite,' she replied. 'It's out of season. It will be lovely.'

'He suggests the last week of April-and then he could come back with me. Easter is really early again this year. I probably could do it.'

'Go for it, Rose. You don't know when you'll get another chance.'

'I'll see what Katie says.'

'Do you mind going on your own?' said Katie when Rose told her.

'No. It's only from Gatwick. There's no difficult changes.'

'I mean, you'll be there on your own,'

'But I was on the coach trips and, anyway, he's promised to show me round.'

'Can you trust him, Mum?'

'I think so. He's been the perfect gentleman. It's only for a week and he's paying for my stay. I only have to pay for the flight.'

'Well, you know him better than we do. If it feels right, book it.'

So she did.

'Katie, do you have a solicitor?' asked Rose when her new passport arrived and she was helping her daughter with Sunday lunch.

'Yes, Bernard and I had our wills made when we bought the house. It's Walpole and Biggs in the village. Walpole is quite old but Biggs is much younger. Why?'

'I'd like to update my will before I go abroad.'

'That's morbid. Nothing is going to happen to you.'

'Nevertheless. I've rather more money than you realise. There's still some left from Lane's End. Naturally I have left most of it to you but I want to add Karen. Young people need so much for college these days. Also, Chantelle wasn't in my old will and I should leave her something. You do understand, don't you?'

'Of course. Whatever you decide is OK by me.'

'James and Chantelle had a very good solicitor in the Lakes. If I can find someone as reliable I shall be content. I'll feel better about the trip if that is settled.'

'Anyone would think you are venturing into the Amazon jungle!'

'Next time, perhaps,' she joked.

When the plane landed at the airport in Malta Rose was pleased to see Major Trent waiting for her.

'No need to go in a taxi,' he said. 'It will be my pleasure to transport you.'

'It feels strange, not being with a group,' said Rose.

'I booked you in for Bed and Breakfast. There are so many lovely restaurants I want you to experience.'

'Better than the food at your hotel?'

'I'm afraid so. Our hotel menu is rather predictable – seeing as we cater largely for the British palate.'

'And you think I might like to try something more adventurous?'

'I'm sure of it. Let's get you booked in. Your room looks out over the bay. I hope you like it.'

It was quite a bare room, Rose thought. There was the minimum of simple furniture a bed, a chest of drawers and a fitted wardrobe. A small TV screen was hanging on the wall above a tiny dressing table. Henry had claimed the hotel had four stars but she couldn't see why.

He was, however, correct about the view from the balcony.

To her left was the hotel swimming pool but to her right was the tiny harbour with a pier jutting out into the turquoise sea.

The air was warm, not hot, and she could just see the road to the rest of the resort winding up the hill away from them. But it was the boats that charmed her. They were unlike any she had seen before, brightly coloured, with a distinctive shape that reminded her of ancient Egyptian drawings.

She breathed in the afternoon air and turned away, reluctant to unpack but aware that Major Trent was waiting for her downstairs.

She changed into white trousers and a patterned top and slung her bag over her shoulder. I hope he didn't want me to dress up for dinner, she thought. I can't do that every night.

'We aren't going far this evening,' he said as he steered her out of the front entrance. 'Just up the hill. It's my favourite restaurant. There are plenty of others, one that does very good pasta dishes, but this one has a choice of really good food.'

'You remembered I like pasta,' said Rose.

'I try,' he smiled. 'As you know - food is a passion of mine.'

Once seated in the restaurant Rose saw what he meant. There were vegetarian, meat and fish dishes, in three different languages, Maltese, English and Italian.

'What do you recommend?' asked Rose.

'The freshly caught bass is very good,' he replied.

'Then I'll have that, with sparkling water please, Henry, and you can surprise me with the dessert.'

'What a lovely idea. You always keep me guessing, Rose. I think this week will be very special.'

'I didn't look much up before I came away but I did see there was a glass factory. That's somewhere I would like to visit.'

'That's on the itinerary already, with a harbour tour and a visit to Mosta Dome.

I hope you've brought your camera.'

'I have, but not the computer, or a tablet. I'll just have to buy lots of postcards.'

By the time the meal was over and they had sampled baklava and had coffee Rose was ready for bed.

'I'm sorry, Henry. I'm very tired from the journey. Could we save any more exploring for another day?' she said.

'Of course. I'll see you back and then take a stroll along the front, if you don't mind. I've had an easy day and I want to check out the boat trips.'

He gave her a quick peck on the cheek and she made her way to her room, too exhausted to do anything but have a quick wash and turn in. The bed was a double and rather hard but she didn't care. All she wanted to do was sleep.

TWELVE

Next morning, at breakfast, she felt a little awkward, sitting alone at a table. There was no sign of Major Trent and she began to feel slightly annoyed.

Then, just as she was about to return to her room he came rushing in.

'My apologies, Rose. I neglected to arrange a meeting time. I have the car outside. How about a drive round the island while we make plans?'

'You'll have to give me a few minutes,' said Rose. 'What do I need to bring?'

'Just a scarf, in case we venture into a church,' said Henry, 'and your camera, of course.'

'I'd like to get my bearings, find where to change money and an information centre.'

'Right, we'll head back at lunchtime and we can have a little siesta, then I'll show you what the bay has to offer. I'll be outside.'

What's the rush? thought Rose, Perhaps he's on a yellow line, or whatever they use to stop parking here in Malta.

She couldn't shake off the feeling of irritation. She hoped Major Trent wasn't going to take over her whole holiday. She needed some time to herself.

Instead, she was whisked round the island, shown various bays, treated to a pea pie in Valletta, where Major Trent extolled the virtues of the little pastizzis and promised to get her to try the ricotta version on another day, and then shown the Mosta Dome where the bomb came through the roof but didn't explode.

She'd been astounded by the narrow streets with their honey coloured houses and their painted wooden balconies. She felt as if she was a time traveller and was surprised so many people spoke English

The hotel had leaflets and brochures about the whole island and, having looked at them, she began to realise that, although it was advertised as a great place for snorkelling, there were very few sandy beaches. She did not fancy climbing down steps into the water, or swimming from a boat.

She bought some postcards and told the Major she needed time to write them on her balcony.

'Righto,' he declared. 'How about I pick you up at three o'clock?'

'Let's say four and I might get in a little nap,' she replied.

'Of course. Forgive me. There's so much I want to show you and so little time.'

* * *

By the weekend Major Trent had taken her to Mdina, called the Silent City because there were almost no vehicles allowed inside the walls, and the glass factory, and given her a boat trip round the harbour that taught her about the siege of the island and ended in a barbecue on shore.

Mdina was awe inspiring, with a beautiful cathedral, full of gold and blue, with coloured frescos that asked to be viewed for longer. It would have been even more enjoyable if she hadn't felt Major Trent hovering at her elbow, waiting to show her something else.

Finally, in the glass factory, she insisted he go and get a drink while she chose presents for the family. She would have liked to stay and watch the craftsmen blowing the glass but she was afraid Henry would interrupt her and she wouldn't have time for shopping.

She bought Maltese cross pendants for Katie and Heather, a glass turtle for herself, just because she loved the smooth feel of its shell when she handled it, and an elegant glass vase for Chantelle. Looking at the light gleaming through the delicate patterning she felt she could wander round in admiration for hours. There were paperweights with swirls of colour, miniature fish that looked as if they belonged in an aquarium, or the Caribbean. She'd never been one for ornaments but these were so beautiful they were hard to resist, until she tried to imagine packing them to fly home.

Friday evening they were back in the local restaurant for dinner and Rose plucked up the courage to tell Major Trent she needed some time to herself.

'It's been wonderful, Henry,' she said. 'And you are the perfect host, but I'm not used to all this activity. I need time to absorb it and I would dearly like one day to, as they say, chill out, on my own.'

'Oh dear, I have been monopolising you, haven't I? I enjoy your company so much. Of course you need time to yourself, but I would still like to take you to the musical evening tomorrow. Would that be enough time?'

Rose laughed. He looked so concerned she felt a wave of sympathy. He must be really lonely when I'm not with him, she thought. He hasn't introduced me to any friends, except the owner of the restaurant.

'Maybe if I can have Saturday to myself I'll be better company for the rest of the holiday,' she replied. She already knew what she wanted to do – take a bus to Mellieha, where there was a sandy beach and have a proper seaside day.

She was beginning to wonder why she never saw him at breakfast, but she hadn't the courage to ask. I suppose it is one of the perks of being the owner, she thought, having breakfast in your room.

She'd missed out on using the pool and promised herself she would do that before she went home. Could it be that Major Trent didn't like swimming?

She put a long cotton skirt on over her swimming costume and packed a change of clothes. She had a broad brimmed straw hat and left her legs bare in strappy sandals. I look like a typical holiday maker, she giggled, as she checked herself in the mirror.

Taking the bus on her own gave her a completely different thrill from being with Major Trent. She had been missing the feeling of control, the release of being able to choose what she did and when, the relief at not having to talk and listen all the time.

She got off the bus and breathed in the salty air. A light breeze was tickling the sand and making it drift into little eddies of dust. She looked round for a less exposed spot but had to settle for the shelter of a wall. That's the problem, she thought, the island has too few trees. I don't think I'll have a picnic lunch. She could taste the sand on her tongue and quickly divested herself of her clothes and made her way to the water's edge.

There were a few people dotted about the beach and a couple of teenagers in the sea but it was surprisingly empty. The sand was soft beneath her feet and there didn't seem to be any rocks to avoid. She walked out until the water was waist high and then plunged in. It was cold at first, but not unpleasantly so, as it would have been in England. She didn't go far, swimming parallel to the beach, and turning to float on her back. Then the sun disappeared behind a cloud and the waves got higher.

She looked back at the beach. The wind had grown stronger and the sand was flying though the air in swirls. People were picking up their belongings and retreating to the road.

As she came out of the water the sand stung the back of her legs. She grabbed her things, wrapped herself in her towel and followed the others off the beach.

There were few buildings by the shore. The road wound steeply up the hill to the village. Most people seemed to have disappeared into a nearby hotel.

Rose dressed quickly in the bus shelter and started to

climb the hill. She needed to find a toilet and, if possible, a hot drink.

'Good morning, lady,' said a voice and a bronzed young man approached her.

'Would you like some refreshment? I am showing people our holiday apartments – no obligation. You only have to look. We hope you will tell your friends back in England? We have free drinks and sandwiches for anyone who views our properties. Please come. I am only paid if I bring someone.'

'I'd like to see them, but I don't want to buy,' she said.

'You only have to take a week. It means you have your own place and can use all the facilities, pools, restaurants, entertainment, all very reasonable, but there's no obligation. Just come and see, please.'

She hadn't the heart to refuse. He seemed so eager, and what harm would it do? She would be somewhere out of the wind and it would be something to tell Major Trent about.

'How far is it?' she asked.

'Just a little way up the hill,' he replied, 'No distance.'

In fact it was almost at the top and made for absolutely stunning views. She could see why the apartments had been built here. The bungalows were terraced and there was a pool on each level.

She was taken into a large reception hall where small tables were set out with piles of coloured brochures. A tall, slim lady approached them. 'Thank you, Donny,' she said and the young man left.

'I'm Jennifer,' she said. 'Would you like a drink before we take the tour?'

'I'd like to use the bathroom first, ' said Rose. 'I've just come off the beach.'

'You are on holiday?' asked Jennifer when Rose returned.

'Yes, but this looks way out of my league. I don't want to waste your time.'

'You may as well see what we have to offer. It is easy to fall in love with Malta and want to come back every year. Of course you can always let family members have your week. It's a great way to ensure you get a the holiday you feel comfortable with.'

As they walked round the complex Rose looked at the residents. They were stretched out on loungers looking, to be honest, rather bored. No-one was chatting, no-one was even smiling. They were surrounded by elegant plants and exotic flowers but they didn't look happy. Even if she could have afforded it, this was not her idea of a good holiday.

'You have family?' asked Jennifer.

'Yes.'

'And do they know Malta?'

'No, they've never been.'

'Well, come and collect one of our brochures and you can tell them all about it.'

Rose was ushered to one of the little tables, brought some pastries and a drink and bombarded with facts and figures. An hour later she made her escape, after only giving the barest of details and a false address.

As she waited for the bus to St Paul's Bay she found she was shivering. She would go back, have a warm bath and go to bed for an hour or so. She was more in need of peace than ever.

* * *

Entering the hotel she found Major Trent sitting in the lounge. He rose to greet her.

'My dear Rose. I didn't expect you back so soon,' he said, leading her to a chair.

'Thank you, Henry,' she replied. 'I do need to sit down. I don't feel very well.'

'Would you like a drink-coffee, tea?'

'I think a coffee would be fine. I must have a chill. I went to Mellieha and was caught by a timeshare tout. They showed me the complex. It was beautifully laid out with flower beds and little pools but the residents looked miserable.'

'You didn't succumb?'

'Oh, no. They couldn't catch me like that. I wouldn't want a timeshare even if I could afford it, and it's on the top of a hill; not somewhere I would want to stay in spite of the views.'

Major Trent ordered the coffees and sat down next to her.

'I'm afraid I have some bad news, too,' he began. 'I won't be coming back to the UK with you. I have to go to Italy on Monday to sort out some paperwork to do with the castle. One can't do everything on line, not when signatures are required.'

'But it's still going through?'

'I hope so. If you like I'll bring the details down later and show you.'

'I don't think I'll be dining tonight. I'll have to cry off our date. I need to get warm and I think I'll stay in my room and hope I can sleep it off.'

'What a pity. Shall I see you tomorrow? It will be our last day together. I was hoping to show you some ruins.'

'I think I'm the ruin at the moment. Let's say ten o'clock, shall we? And if I'm not better I'll leave a message at the desk.'

She finished her coffee and walked slowly to the lift. Major Trent looked defeated. Whatever he had planned for that evening, she just wasn't up to it. In fact, she felt ready to go home.

Next morning Rose woke feeling lethargic but otherwise well.

She determined to enjoy her breakfast and be as polite to Major Trent as possible. She understood why he had tried to pack so many new experiences into one week and, most of the time, she had been content in his company.

I'll have some great memories, she thought, but now I want a rest.

It seemed as if Major Trent had finally realised that it was impossible to show her everything in so short a time.

'I've changed my mind about today,' he said. 'The hotel we were going to last night for the musical evening is just about the best on the island. It isn't on the beach, it's inland, but the food is excellent. I have booked a table for lunch. Otherwise I am at your disposal.'

'I did wonder about the glass bottomed boats,' she said.

'If you feel up to it. The sea is pretty calm right now and we can do it from here in the bay.'

So she followed him to the end of the pier and they joined the other holidaymakers on a small boat.

It was a little disappointing. They did see some fish but it wasn't quite as exciting as she had imagined. She found herself thinking about home, the flat, the shop and her family. I'm glad I came, she thought. I have plenty to tell them.

Major Trent took her back to the hotel and she finally had the chance to change into the embroidered cotton maxi dress she had bought for the trip. If the hotel was as posh as he had indicated she wouldn't look out of place.

Rose ordered a salad and Henry had beef stew. He ordered a bottle of local wine and she had a small glass but it felt peculiar, to her, to be drinking wine at lunchtime. It certainly didn't go with the creamy confection they were served with to complete the meal.

'Coffee?' suggested Major Trent.

'Yes, please,' she said, 'but I must warn you, I need to have a siesta when I get back to the hotel.'

'But I'll see you this evening?'

'Maybe. As the shops open late I'd like to do a bit of last minute shopping.'

'You are dining in the hotel?'

'Why not? Henry, you have been very odd about eating there.'

'I'm sorry. It's just that we were fined for not being up to scratch. I didn't want anything to happen to you. It was last season and we had a deep clean and changed the chef. Nobody has been ill this year but I didn't want to risk it.'

'You could have told me. I have been having breakfast every day.'

'I know. I'm sorry. This time of year there's very little likelihood of a problem. It's when the weather gets really hot.'

'That's why you go back to Cornwall.'

'Not the only reason – but that gives me the chance to tell you my plans for this summer. I can't bear the thought of not seeing you again, Rose, so I contacted a friend of mine who has a boat, not a fancy yacht, just a little boat he uses for trips along the coast and over to France.'

'The boat is in England?'

'Yes, it's moored at Shoreham. He's going to let me use it for a couple of weeks in August, just as a base, if you haven't got tired of me. Would that be acceptable?'

'You mean, you'd stay on the boat so that you could visit me?'

'Yes. I wouldn't expect you to take time off but we could meet up when you weren't busy, couldn't we? I don't know that part of the country so I could do a bit of exploring.'

Rose struggled to decide how she felt about the suggestion. She had been steeling herself to say goodbye to Major Trent and this was a surprise. She really liked being with him but didn't want him to get so attached to her that he wanted to make it a permanent arrangement. Still, two weeks in August wasn't a marriage proposal, was it?

'I'm sure Katie and Chantelle would love to meet you,' she said, at last. 'I've told them so much about you.'

'Your family sound lovely,' he said, looking relieved. 'Now, I must show you the plans for the castle before you go home.'

'How about we meet at the pizza restaurant? I want to try their spaghetti carbonara – but I might need to share one with you. They serve such large helpings.'

Henry laughed and she considered him fondly. He's fine in small doses, she thought.

Lying on her bed in the hotel that afternoon Rose found she couldn't sleep. Was there a way she could keep Major Trent in her life without him wanting more? If he lived nearby it would be simple. She could see him once or twice a week, maybe cook him a meal, or go to the theatre together. She would like him in her life but could not see how they were going to manage it. She would wait until she got home. Everything might seem different, then.

THIRTEEN

'Thank goodness you're back,' said Chantelle when Rose had unpacked her things and joined her in the shop

'Why, what's up?'

'I think one of the staff has been taking things home without paying, but I don't know which one.'

'How do you know?'

'I've seen things being unpacked that just don't get on the hangers.'

'Have you reported it?'

'No. I was waiting for you. Between us we can probably catch the culprit.'

'What kind of things?'

'Children's stuff – but nobody here has young children.'

'Grandchildren,' said Rose. 'Two of them have grand-children.'

*   *   *

It took a week with both of them waiting and watching before the latest volunteer, a lady of about sixty, called Deirdre, proved to be the thief.

She was about to leave one afternoon when Chantelle challenged her.

'Have you seen the little pinafore dress that came in this morning?' she asked. 'I saw you ironing it.'

'Pinafore dress? Someone must have bought it.'

'You didn't sell it, then?'

'I don't remember.'

'Is it possible you might have picked it up by mistake?'

Deirdre flushed bright red. 'I don't think so.'

'Well, how about looking through your bag, just in case?'

She hesitated and then slowly explored her bag. Inside, unwrapped, was the child's pinafore dress.

'Oh dear,' stuttered Deirdre. 'It must have dropped in there while I was at the till.'

'Really?' said Chantelle. 'And is it the only thing?'

'I don't understand.'

'I think you do. I would rather you did not return, as a volunteer or a customer. I might have to involve the police.'

Deirdre tried to look insulted but hurriedly put her belongings back in her bag and left, saying nothing.

Rose, who had been watching, said, 'You let her off too lightly. You should have had her arrested.'

'I know. I hadn't the heart. I'll put ten quid in the till to make up for what we've lost. Maybe we should have a camera in here.'

'Don't ask for one yet. I'm sure everyone else is honest.'

'But folk do take stuff, Rose. It's too easy.'

'How about a mirror over the door?'

'Yes, that would help. Thanks, Rose.'

That evening Chantelle was checking the emails when she called to Rose.

'You've got an email, from a Daniel Curtis,' she said. 'Come and see.'

Rose came out of the kitchen and peered over Chantelle's shoulder.

'It's the photographer,' she said, delightedly. 'He's having an exhibition of his work in Chichester.'

'There, you see. He has remembered you.'

'It's next week and he's asked me to go.'

'You'll have to go on Monday when we are closed. A day in Chichester. What a treat.'

'Why don't you come, too? He wouldn't mind. He's a very sympathetic and generous person.'

'How old is he?'

'About your age – too young for me,' she laughed.

'Don't you go matchmaking,' said Chantelle. 'I've spent enough time with a man, but I would like to see his pictures. You could always tell me to get lost if I was in the way.'

'You won't be,' said Rose. 'I'm so pleased he's been in touch.'

'Well, sit down and write a reply,' ordered Chantelle. 'We can go on the train and make a day of it.'

* * *

Rose always felt a little intimidated by Chichester, or 'Chi' as the locals called it. Being the County Town it seemed to have an air of importance and it was the cultural centre of the district with the cathedral, the theatre and a thriving college.

Daniel's photographs were being displayed in a small gallery just off the main shopping street.

They arrived at about eleven o'clock and found only two other people walking round inside.

Rose looked for the pictures of Cornwall and was pleased to see the photo she had suggested of the window box in Port Isaac. There were some of waves breaking on a beach and a number of sunset shots, including one of the remains of the mine workings, but the one of the window box was her favourite.

A few of the photographs had 'sold' stickers next to them.

Chantelle was looking at some scenes of hills and moorlands. 'Look at the colour of the heather in this one,' she said to Rose. 'It looks like a purple sea.'

'And birds,' said Rose, 'That one of geese flying across the sky. He's really good, isn't he?'

'I'm glad you said that,' came a warm voice from behind her. 'Hallo, Rose.'

'Daniel!' she almost shrieked. 'These are wonderful. I knew they would be.'

Daniel laughed. 'Are you going to introduce me?' nodding at Chantelle.

'Oh, yes, Daniel, this is Chantelle, Chantelle, this is the fantastic photographer.'

Chantelle held out her hand and Daniel shook it.

'Rose does go overboard, doesn't she?' he said.

'Rightly so. I'm no expert but some of these are stunning.'

'Only some?' he joked.

Chantelle did not rise to the challenge. 'Where did you take these?' she asked.

'In the Lake District; why, do you know it?'

'I lived there for quite a long time, but now I live with Rose.'

'I should have told you,' said Rose. 'We have a flat over a charity shop. Perhaps you'd like to come over to tea one day?'

'I'd like that, but how about I shut up shop now and take you two ladies to lunch. Monday is a very quiet day and we have to eat.'

'That would be great,' replied Rose, 'and when we come back there's a picture I'd like to look at again.'

'I think you may have made a sale,' said Chantelle.

'There's no obligation,' said Daniel. Rose winced. She'd heard that phrase before and it reminded her of Malta.

They lunched in a local pub and Daniel told them what he'd been doing since Cornwall, how the magazine liked the Cornish pictures and he had been asked to do some of Scotland and the North East, how his picture of puffins had won a prize in a competition and how his next job was to take photos of a stately home.

'The best commission I had was at a zoo,' he said. 'I loved doing close-ups of the animals, especially the giraffe. Nobody really examines a giraffe's face, they just see the long legs and neck.'

'Are some of them here, on show?' asked Rose.

'Yes, but they're sold.'

'I wasn't going to buy one,' she replied. 'It's just that we never had time to see everything before you whisked us off for lunch.'

'It's not often I get the chance to entertain two lovely ladies,' he said. 'How long have you got?'

'As long as we like,' said Chantelle. 'When we've seen the pictures there's some shopping I'd like to do.'

'Why don't you shop first and come back later?' he said. 'There's plenty of seats in the back room. You might need one.'

'Well, I will,' said Rose. 'My old legs give out after a while.'

'Thanks, Daniel,' said Chantelle, 'and if your exhibition is over by next Monday we'd love to see you at the flat. There's street parking outside. I'll send you details on email. Say, three thirty?'

'Make it two thirty,' said Rose, 'then we'll miss the schools coming out.'

'Two thirty, then. That's a date,' said Daniel. 'I'll see you both later, happy shopping.'

'He's very nice, Rose,' said Chantelle once they were back out on the street. 'I can see why you like him.'

'He makes me laugh,' said Rose. 'I don't know why. He's just relaxing.'

'You make him sound like a hot chocolate.'

'More like a hot bath,' said Rose and giggled. 'Now, what are we shopping for?'

'A new electric kettle and a cover for the ironing board, and I'd like some new undies. We couldn't do that with a man around.'

'What? Not cheap cotton ones from the market?'

'No, not any more. I want something a bit prettier.'

'Why? It's only me and you that see them.'

'I want them for me, that's allowed, isn't it? James couldn't care less what I wore but I've lost a bit of weight and I feel I deserve some nice underwear.'

'You do, Chantelle. Which reminds me, we need to find a doctor now we are settled.'

'I know, but don't let's talk about it now. There's a department store. We can get everything in one place.'

Back at the gallery they took time admiring each photograph until Rose said, 'That's enough. It's all I can handle. I must sit down Daniel, I need to talk to you.'

'Yes, Rose.'

'The photo of the window box. I'd like to buy it.'

'I'll have to charge you for the frame but the picture will always be yours, Rose. It was your idea.'

'Thank you.' She didn't argue. She'd seen two other people buy pictures in the short time they had been there. He wasn't a struggling artist, but he was a good friend.

That became even more obvious when he offered to keep hold of their purchases until he saw them the following week.

'I guess we can boil water in a saucepan 'till then,' said Chantelle. 'Or borrow the kettle from downstairs.'

'I'll bring the picture and the kettle,' said Daniel.

'We'll be off, then,' said Rose. 'I'm beginning to feel my age.'

'Should I run you to the station?'

'No, it's all right. I'll get a sit down on the train. Thanks for a lovely day, Daniel.'

'See you soon,' he said. 'Bye, Chantelle.'

'Bye, Daniel.'

Chantelle had told Mrs Dunn about the theft but she didn't seem very surprised. 'Next time, consider informing the authorities,' she said, 'but in your shoes I probably would have done the same.'

Now they were were planning the Monday tea.

'Sandwiches, I think,' said Rose. 'Ham and tomato, cheese and pickle and egg and cress.'

'Is he a vegetarian?' asked Chantelle.

'I don't think so. He didn't say so when we were in Cornwall.'

'You must make one of your victoria sponges,' said Chantelle.

'And a chocolate cake. Men like chocolate.'

'How about shortbread? That would be nice if he stays later.'

'Do you think he might? Should we get in some sherry, or beer?'

'We'll get both. I can always drink the beer and you do like an odd sherry.'

'And I can do a quiche. If we don't eat it on Monday it will do for later in the week.'

'Brilliant. I just hope he doesn't mind eating in the kitchen.'

'He didn't seem the sort to care.'

Two thirty, on the dot, Daniel drove into the parking space in front of the shop.

Chantelle ran down the stairs to let him in.

'This is a handy part of town,' he said, 'and the shop looks great.'

'It was all redecorated before we moved in,' said Chantelle, 'but Joyce does make a good job of the window.' She glanced over at the toys and books on little shelves behind some colourful bric-a-brac, jigsaw puzzles and a delicate tea set.

At the top of the stairs Rose greeted them with a cheery, 'Hallo, Daniel.'

'Hi, Rose, How's things? Here's your kettle.'

'Fine, Daniel, good to see you. If you two go in the lounge I'll be with you in a minute,' and she retreated to the kitchen.

Daniel walked up to the large window looking out over the rear of the property.

'You can't see the sea from here,' he said. 'I'm a bit inland, too, in a village near Bognor. It isn't half as convenient as here.'

'What made you end up there? I'd have though you would want to be in London?'

'Not when I can do so much of my work on the internet. But my wife worked at the big house.'

'You're married?'

'I was. She died of cancer three years ago. I have one daughter, but she's in Canada.'

'You must miss her.'

'I do, but you go where your partner goes, don't you?'

'I certainly did,' Chantelle agreed. 'I had to elope. Bernard's father was much older than me.'

'But you had a lot in common?'

'Oh, yes. That's how we ended up making greetings cards. I've still got a few examples. Would you like to see them?'

'After tea,' said Rose from the doorway. 'I've got the kettle on. It works. I'm afraid we've got no table in here so we eat in the kitchen, Daniel.'

'I don't even have a kitchen,' said Daniel. 'I'm in a studio flat. I share a bathroom. This place is a palace in comparison.'

When they had finished tea, Chantelle brought out a folder of James's art work, pictures of animals and landscapes and pages of rhymes, examples of card and a selection of different coloured ribbons.

'They were all hand made,' said Chantelle.

'Who did the calligraphy?'

'I did. I put them together. It was a joint effort.'

'James was a perfectionist,' said Daniel. 'I wish I had that talent. I can see a picture but I can't reproduce it.'

'What you do is just as artistic,' said Rose, 'What are you working on next?'

'London scenes,' he replied, 'But they have to be unique, not Big Ben or St. Paul's.'

'How will you do that?' asked Chantelle.

'I know,' said Rose, 'with close-ups.'

'Exactly. I'll find an alleyway or a door that nobody has noticed. It will be an adventure.'

'Like photographing part of a bridge instead of a whole bridge?' said Chantelle.

'That's it. I'm looking forward to it.'

'And no more coach trips?' said Rose.

'Not this year - and that reminds me, how's Major Trent?'

So Rose told them about Malta and they hardly noticed it getting dark.

'Goodness,' said Daniel, at last. 'I must be going. I've taken up much too much of your time.'

'I'll get you a coffee,' said Rose. 'I suppose it's too late for another drink.'

'Coffee would be fine, Rose. I'm not much of a drinker- but I would like to take both of you out to dinner one evening, when I return from London. There's a lovely country pub that does really good food and it's lonely eating on my own.'

'We'd love that,' said Rose. 'Wouldn't we, Chantelle?'

'Yes, thank you.'

'And Chantelle can tell you all about her line dancing,' said Rose, mischievously.

'Stop it, Rose. It's just a bit of fun.' Chantelle blushed.

'To really good music, I suppose,' said Daniel.

'Country- I prefer folk but it's a happy sound and folk songs can be quite miserable.'

'Agreed. I'll have to play you some of my CD's one day.'

Their conversation was interrupted by the coffee and when Daniel left they had the feeling they could easily have spent even more time together.

It was the last week in November when Chantelle began to pack up her computer and asked Terry to dispose of it for her.

'I'm changing it for a new laptop and printer,' she told Rose. 'I need the space on my desk.'

'What for?'

'It's Daniel's fault. He got me thinking about Christmas cards and I realised I didn't have to use paintings, I could use photographs.'

'So you asked him to provide some?'

'Got it in one. He had loads on line and then he sent me four to choose from and I'm going to make some and sell them in the shop.'

'It's a bit late, isn't it?'

'Yes. That's why I must get on with it. Which ones do you think?'

Rose examined the four prints. One was a snowy scene with a church, one was a close-up of coloured baubles, one was starlings flying over a pier and one was of two mince pies and a drink set out on a table.

'That's typical Daniel,' said Rose. 'A treat for Santa.'

'Yes, I'll choose that, and the baubles and the church. The starlings are very atmospheric but not really Christmassy.'

'Keep them for another time. I think they'll be very popular.'

When the invitation from Daniel came, Rose was half inclined to tell Chantelle she couldn't go but, instead, vowed to try to judge whether the two of them were getting close.

They had met up at least once, to discuss the cards and Chantelle had brought examples to show him.

They got a taxi to the restaurant in the country hotel

and Daniel was there to greet them.

Rose looked at the ivy covered frontage with its imposing portico.

'It's a bit posh, Daniel,' she said.

'This is my Christmas present to you both,' said Daniel. 'I've been very lucky this year and have some more good news. Let's get inside and I'll tell you.'

Rose looked at the extensive menu, hoping to find something she recognised.

'I think I'll pass on the starter,' she said. 'I'll have the chicken.'

'And white wine?' asked Daniel.

'Yes, please,' said Chantelle. 'Nothing too strong.'

'There's meringue on the menu, Rose,' teased Daniel.

'I know, but I thought of having the Christmas pudding.'

'With brandy sauce!' declared Chantelle, 'You'll be drunk as a skunk.'

It was a jolly party and Rose quite forgot she was supposed to be looking for signs that they were getting close, until Daniel said,

'I've a new commission for next year. I have to photograph country houses for a prestigious magazine. They saw my work on London and got in touch. It's the most important booking I have ever had.'

'That's wonderful,' said Chantelle. 'You'll be travelling all over the country.'

'Is it the National Trust?' asked Rose.

'No, it's a property firm that only deals in country houses.'

'Not Riverbridge Properties?'

'Not likely. This is way out of their league.'

'I'm so happy for you,' said Chantelle and Rose watched as she put her hand on his arm and leaned towards him. Did he look surprised or delighted?

He glanced at Rose and squeezed Chantelle's hand.

'You were going to show me the cards,' he said.

'After dinner,' she replied. 'They aren't as good as I used to do. It's hard with only one hand but at least I've still got the one I write with.'

'And she still types faster than I do with two hands,' said Rose.

'I think you're both amazing,' said Daniel, diplomatically.

I'm right, thought Rose. They do have feelings for each other. This is the last time I act as a gooseberry, and she couldn't help smiling. She expected to feel jealous but she just felt pleased as if she had been instrumental in bringing happiness to two people she loved, because she did love both of them, in different ways. They weren't family but they had given her their trust and become an important part of her life.

CHAPTER
FOURTEEN

Christmas with Katie and Bernard was a joyous occasion, especially as they had a video link with Robbie from Australia.

He'd applied and been accepted as a permanent resident and was engaged to an Australian athlete who was hoping to go to the Olympic Games.

'He's really got himself into the swing of things, out there, Mum,' said Katie. 'He looks so well.'

'It's all that outdoor living,'said Rose. 'I thought he'd never find a girl friend. He just seemed so fond of sheep.'

'Maybe she looks like a sheep,' laughed Bernard.

'As long as she loves him, I don't care,' responded Katie, 'But it's a long way to go for a wedding.'

'Would you?' asked Rose.

'I'd like to. We'll just have to wait and see.'

* * *

Rose was also waiting to hear when Major Trent was coming to Shoreham.

She hadn't really missed him. It had been a busy time, but as the year went on she began to wonder about his plans.

Then, in February, she had an email from him. 'I'm in Blackpool. I'm not going to Malta this year. I'll be at the boat the first two weeks of March. Look forward to seeing you. Henry.'

'That's your Valentine, Rose,' said Chantelle.

'I see you didn't get one,' replied Rose.

'Maybe I did and maybe I didn't,' said Chantelle. 'That's for youngsters, anyway. Who would send me one?'

'Chantelle, you can't kid me. Daniel, of course.'

'I haven't seen him for weeks.'

'And you haven't been in touch?'

'That's different.'

'When's he back?'

'Before Easter. Perhaps we can make a foursome with the Major?'

'Perhaps.' That might be a good idea, she thought. I'm not sure about being alone on a boat with Major Trent.

'You've shaved off your moustache!' she exclaimed when Major Trent turned up at the shop.

'And you noticed,' he replied. 'So this is your establishment.'

He looked over at Chantelle, standing by the till.

'You must be Chantelle,' he said. 'Rose has told me so much about you.'

'Ditto,' said Chantelle. 'I'm pleased to meet you, Major Trent.'

'Is it permitted to take your assistant out to lunch?' he enquired.

'Of course.' She grinned at Rose.

'Come upstairs, Henry,' said Rose. 'I need to get my things.'

She felt flustered, having the Major in her home. Somehow she had kept him compartmentalised as a holiday experience.

She must admit he did look good, younger than before and still smartly dressed. Where would he suggest for lunch?

'The public house on the corner or Chinese?' asked Major Trent when they left the shop.

'The pub has a good reputation, although I haven't been in.'

'There's a first time for everything, Rose.'

She asked for a cheese and ham baguette and then regretted it. This was something she could not eat elegantly.

Major Trent had soup and his eyes twinkled as he watched her.

'It's good to see you again, Rose,' he said. She couldn't reply. She had her mouth full.

'That's a very nice flat you have there,' he continued.

'We rent it, from the charity,' she said at last.

'And your mobile home?'

'I sold it. I'm staying here for good.'

'I must admit I'm beginning to think I should find somewhere permanent.'

'In Blackpool?'

'Maybe – but there's so much to sort out.'

'The castle in Italy?'

'That is proving to be a problem. We have paid the initial deposit, seventy thousand pounds, and now we have cash flow issues. We need to find the rest by September or we forfeit the sale. It wouldn't be so bad but they have the right to ask for double the deposit if we renege.'

'That doesn't seem fair.'

'We thought we had an investor who would come in with us but they pulled out. I had plans for a cookery school and writing and painting holidays. It would have been wonderful.'

'But your company is in trouble?'

'Celia and I weren't doing it through the company. We were investing for our retirement. We were going to sell the company.'

'Surely you'll have plenty of money then?'

'The bank didn't see it like that, but never mind, that's my problem, not yours. Don't let's spoil our time together.'

'How's the boat?'

'Just as rough as usual. Would you like to come on Sunday and see it? We wouldn't have to stay on it. We could eat out.'

'I usually have lunch with the family. I could come at about three.'

'I'll come and pick you up if you tell me where you'll be.'

'I'd like that. They're very curious about you.'

'Then I'll have to be on my best behaviour,' he joked.

* * *

159

'Take your camera, Mum,' said Katie when Rose explained that Major Trent was picking her up from the Meadows.

'Should I? You don't think he'll think it a little odd?'

'Everyone does it all the time. They even take pictures of the food they are eating.'

'But they do that with a phone, not a camera.'

'You know my answer to that.'

'I suppose I could have invited him to join us for lunch.'

'Not yet. Wait until you know him better. He doesn't seem the type to muck in with families.'

'I suppose he's not – and I don't know anyone military to make him feel at home.'

'He can come in for a coffee and we'll try not to frighten him off,' said Katie. 'Chantelle has already told me she can't come.'

'I think she's seeing Daniel. They seem to be an item.'

'Good. They're well matched.'

'As long as she doesn't want to move out. I couldn't manage on my own.'

'Do you think she might?'

'Not really. They seem quite happy as they are.' It's the kind of arrangement I would like, she thought, but it doesn't look likely if Major Trent wants to retire to Italy.

She'd been learning to cook some Italian dishes at her evening class. It would have been nice, she thought, to do it in their country of origin.

Major Trent arrived on Sunday afternoon with a bunch of flowers for Katie.

He accepted her offer of coffee and asked Bernard about the wooden artefacts he had made.

When Bernard told them he had to go bowling Major Trent asked if he could accompany him and watch and Rose decided to go with them.

The bowling green was situated between the churchyard and the recreation ground. It had a wooden changing room that it shared with the nearby tennis courts.

The green square was bordered by a ditch and then a grass topped wall.

The bowlers were all men, mostly over fifty but there was one young boy who stood out because of his lanky frame and eager expression, as if he couldn't wait to prove his ability.

On the bench overlooking the green sat a couple of elderly ladies and Rose could see movement in the Pavilion that indicated there were more people inside.

'We are only practising today,' said the portly man she took to be the captain. He turned to Major Trent. 'How about having a go?'

'Come on, Major,' coaxed Bernard, and was delighted when he agreed.

Rose could hardly believe how easily he fitted in with the other bowlers. When they invited him to join in it was clear that he was no novice.

Not only did he bowl near to the jack, he also had the skill to knock an opponent's bowl out of the way.

'That was an eye-opener,' she said, as they drove away from the park.

'I've hidden depths,' he replied with a smile. 'What a great bunch of lads.'

'You could join them if you lived here,' she said, without thinking.

'It might come to that,' he muttered.

It was late in the afternoon when Rose and Major Trent reached Shoreham.

The boat was a surprise. It was old, needed painting and had the name 'Maid Marion' on the bow.

She's in need of care and attention, thought Rose, and followed the Major into the cramped cabin below, sneaking a quick snap of him as he bent to go through the door.

Here again, it did not feel as if it was somewhere Major Trent belonged. In fact there were traces of a female influence. Would a military man have cushions on the bunks? Was the friend who owned the boat really a woman? she wondered.

Major Trent hurriedly opened a small cupboard and put two mugs away. There had obviously been someone else on board quite recently.

Rose could see he was uncomfortable and impatient to take her out. It had been a shock to find that he was so unprepared. He had always seemed so efficient and single minded.

She tried to analyse her own reaction to the possibility that she wasn't the only woman in his life. She was hurt, but not exactly jealous. She hadn't wanted his complete attention, had she? She was just annoyed that he had not confided in her.

Their connection had been too limited. She needed to find out more about him.

'I'll wait on the bank, shall I?' she said, and he gave her a nod of assent.

She took one picture of the outside of the boat but hid the camera in her bag when he came up from the cabin and walked her along the river.

'Shoreham's not like Cornwall, is it?' he asked.

'No, but it's pretty self contained,' replied Rose, 'and you know there is a rescue centre for dogs nearby?'

'I do, but I can't say I've ever felt the need for one,' said the Major.

That's a black mark against you, thought Rose, remembering how her family had always loved dogs.

Dinner was pleasant enough but she longed for them to share something else besides meals.

'What kind of music do you like, Henry?' she asked.

'Light classical, big bands, the old stuff.'

'There's a big band playing at the Pavilion next week. Would you like to go?'

'I would, if you would come with me.'

'I'll get the tickets. It will be my treat. They are on at 7pm Friday night.'

'I'll pick you up at the flat, shall I?'

'Yes, it isn't far. Walking is better because the parking isn't brilliant.'

'You'll have eaten?'

'Yes, I'll have a quick bite after the shop closes. I won't need any supper.'

As soon as she had spoken she felt sorry. Major Trent did seem to enjoy his food – but there was more to life than filling your stomach. She wanted to find out what other interests he had. How much did they really have in common?

* * *

'How did it go?' asked Chantelle when she arrived home.

'All right,' said Rose. 'He seemed a bit more serious than when we last met.'

'Miserable serious or serious about you?'

'Worried serious. I think he's got money trouble.'

'Aha!'

'Don't you start. Katie is bad enough.'

'I bet he asked you for money.'

'No, he didn't, but his purchase of the castle is in peril.'

'So he says. I hope you didn't offer to help.'

'I didn't – but I might.'

'Oh, Rose, be careful.'

'I'm not stupid, Chantelle. I wouldn't give money away until I'd seen that the place existed.'

'You'd go to Italy?'

'Why not? I went to Malta.'

'Has he asked you to?'

'No, but I'm seeing him on Friday and thinking of suggesting it. Then we'll see what he says.'

'I bet he doesn't offer to pay this time.'

'I'd be more suspicious if he did.'

'Talk it over with Katie.'

'I will not. What I do with my time and money is my concern – not my daughter's.'

She could hardly concentrate on the music at the concert. She had on a new royal blue trouser suit and had been to the hairdressers in her lunch hour. The band was a little too loud for her but she could see Major Trent was enjoying it, stamping his feet to the marches and applauding the lady soloist with enthusiasm.

By the interval she could wait no longer.

'Henry,' she began, 'I've been thinking.'

'You'd like supper after all?'

'No, it's not that. I'd like to help you set up your castle.'

'I couldn't let you do that. What if it wasn't a success?'

'You believe in it, don't you?'

'Yes.'

'And your hotels are successful, aren't they?'

'Yes.'

'Well. How much do you need to secure the property?'

'We have borrowed most of what we need but there's a twenty thousand pound shortfall.'

'What if I supply the twenty thousand? Would you get it?'

'There are a few commissions to pay, but we could probably manage those. Would you really like to invest?'

'Only if I could come out and see the place for myself. I wouldn't put money into anything I hadn't seen.'

'You'd come out to Tuscany?'

'If that was possible. Is it?'

'I'd have to find you a farmhouse to stay in. That would be the most reasonable way of doing it.'

'Or you tell me where it is and I'll arrange it myself. You won't have to do anything except be there at the same time.'

'Why, Rose, I've never seen you so authoritative.'

'I can be, when I know what I want. What do you say?'

'I'll give you some dates as soon as I can. I must tell Celia. We'll need to get some papers drawn up if you are going to be a co-owner.'

'Don't rush me, Henry, finish your drink. The bell has gone for the second half. Let's relax and enjoy the concert.'

Neither of them seemed absorbed by the music and Rose was glad when it finished.

Henry took her arm as they walked down the steps from the theatre.

'Rose,' he said at the same time as Rose said 'Henry,' and they both laughed nervously.

'Go on,' said Rose.

'I think you should consider what you have offered very carefully. You have to be sure.'

'I've not offered anything yet. I could give you twenty thousand but only if I thought it was something I wanted to be involved with.'

'You'd help get it going?'

'Well, I'd like to spend time there, help with the students or guests or whatever once you get started, until it gets too much for me.'

'That's wonderful. I don't feel so bad about accepting your offer, now,' he said. 'Rose, you are a beautiful woman,' and he turned towards her and enveloped her in a strong embrace.

Rose relaxed into his arms and gave a sigh. When was the last time she had felt a man's arms around her? It was enough. It lifted her spirits and made her certain she was doing the right thing.

Henry released her but kept holding her hand as if she might run away. He was humming one of the tunes that the band had played.

She smiled up at him. 'Life is full of surprises, isn't it?' she said.

'And sometimes,' said Major Trent, 'they are good ones.'

Rose's trip was to be in June and although Chantelle offered to buy her tickets on line Rose insisted on using a travel agent.

'I want to be sure everything is safe,' she said. 'I want the tickets in my hands, and all the insurance details.'

'You'd better be the same about the hotel,' said Chantelle. 'I warn you, Rose. It could be a scam.'

'Stop it, Chantelle. You've met him. You know I've been in all of his hotels already. Sometimes you just have to trust your instincts.'

'I must admit it does look very romantic. Fancy, a cookery school in a real castle in the Tuscan countryside. I'd be ready to go.'

'I wonder if he'll do honeymoons?'

'Rose, I don't know anyone who's planning a wedding, do you?'

'I just wondered.'

'Well don't. Daniel and I are happy as we are, and don't get stars in your eyes or you'll be cheated out of your life's savings.'

'I've booked into the Agriturismo that Henry recommended and he's meeting me at the airport. I've alerted the bank and told my new solicitor what I might be doing. It's as watertight as it can be at this stage.'

'What did the solicitor say?'

'He hoped I was taking someone with me.'

'I wish you were. Don't sign anything you don't understand.'

'Stop spoiling it, Chantelle. I know what I'm doing.'

CHAPTER
FIFTEEN

The heat hit her as soon as she got off the plane. She was glad to get inside the air-conditioned airport building. Major Trent was waiting as promised and loaded her case into a large people carrier.

'That looks useful, Henry,' she said.

'We're getting there,' he replied with a cheerful grin. 'I'm based in the same agriturismo as you. You'll love it.'

The stone farmhouse was set in lush countryside. Rose saw tall trees, vines, olive groves and rolling hills. The air was fresh and if green had a scent, this was it.

'What a lovely place to live,' she said.

'And just you wait until you taste the food,' said Major Trent. 'There's nowhere like it – and tomatoes to die for.'

Rose laughed. 'Food really is your passion, isn't it?'

'And what's wrong with that?'

'Nothing. I like it. I like to hear you being enthusiastic.'

'Then you'll love the castle. Oh, Rose, I'm so glad you're here.'

Rose thrilled at the warmth in his voice. This was an adventure she was going to enjoy. There was no-one here to put a brake on her emotions. It was time she had the freedom to go where her heart led her, even if it was in a very unexpected direction.

By the time she reached her room she felt rather breathless. The agriturismo was high up in the hills and she had to climb quite a few stairs before she sat down on the little single bed. The place was like a rabbit warren and she hoped she could find her way back downstairs. The bathroom was en-suite and looked as if it was shared with another room but when she tried the door it was locked.

I'm glad about that, she thought. I don't want a visitor in the night.

She changed into a light summer dress and picked up her cardigan. She considered leaving her legs bare in her strappy sandals but reckoned it would get cooler later so she stayed in her tights.

Henry was waiting downstairs with a jug of fresh lemonade.

'I've booked a table in the village,' he said. 'We can go when you're ready.'

'Just let me have some time to get adjusted,' she replied. 'How about we sit on the terrace?'

Major Trent nodded at a couple already enjoying the view and held her arm as she sat down.

'I'm sorry,' he said. 'Perhaps you are too tired?'

'No,' she answered irritably. 'I just need a little rest. I don't feel hungry yet.'

Major Trent did not respond. He stared out over the countryside.

I've upset him, she thought, but I won't be bullied.

Eventually she took his hand. 'Thanks, Henry,' she said, 'Let's visit the restaurant. I'll just have one course.'

He took her hand and smiled. 'We have three days,' he said. 'I want you to taste the best this area has to offer.'

He's forgotten I don't drink much, she thought, as Henry ordered a bottle of red wine.

She'd opted for pizza, knowing full well that he'd probably have to help her with it.

'Tell them, a small one,' she said.

'I did better than that,' said Henry. 'I ordered a large one and we can have half each.'

But half a pizza was more than Rose could manage, although it was so different from the ones at home she could hardly believe it. The topping was deep and moist and the base, although crisp, was not hard and tasteless as in Britain. All the vegetables and tomato seemed extra fresh and the cheese was delicious.

'I didn't know pizza could taste like this!' she exclaimed.

'It's good, isn't it?' said Henry. 'More wine, Rose?'

'No, thank you, Henry. It's been a busy day. I don't want to feel dizzy.'

'Coffee, then?'

'No, thank you. If you don't mind I'd rather get back. We have a big day tomorrow.'

'Of course. I hope you sleep well.'

'I'm sure of it.' But she wasn't. She was tired, true, but

the thought of what the next day might bring could easily keep her awake.

Breakfast consisted of fruit and pastries, with a nod to other continentals in the form of cold meats and bread.

Rose had a large glass of orange juice and was happy when Major Trent joined her for coffee.

'Good morning, my dear,' he said. 'It looks like a beautiful day.'

Indeed, the weather was fine and, as she packed her camera, Rose felt a shiver of excitement. The photos of the castle had been impressive and she couldn't wait to see the inside for herself.

The car followed a winding road, bordered by the tall, slim cypress trees, to the top of a hill.

When they alighted she had to take a photo of the view and when Major Trent went over to another man who she assumed was the agent, she took a quick snap of the two of them talking together.

'The owners are not in residence at present,' he told her, 'but the agent has the keys. Do come inside.'

She looked up at the square stone wall. When Henry had first called it a castle she had imagined crenellations but this just looked like an enormous block of stone. The windows were smaller than she would have liked. She tried to imagine it as a hotel, then followed the two men through the entrance to a stone flagged hall.

The place was really sumptuous. There were wood panelled walls, fancy rugs on the floor and what looked to Rose like antique chairs and tables set out as if for a party.

'This is massive,' she gasped.

'Come through. I'll show you the bedrooms,' said the agent. 'There's seven in all and two bathrooms.'

As she climbed the marble staircase Rose knew there would be a four poster bed in at least one room and she wasn't wrong. It was beautifully carved and covered in a silky looking bedspread.

They finished the tour in the kitchen, a space big enough to seat a dozen with room to spare and three ovens and two hobs.

'There's everything you might need,' she said, looking at the copper pots hanging from the ceiling.

'Isn't it perfect?' said Major Trent. 'Now can you see why I was so keen to have it?'

'There's no pool,' said the agent, 'but plenty of room outside if you wanted one.'

'It's beautiful,' said Rose, 'and there's a cellar as well?'

'Of course,' said Major Trent. 'This is a castle after all, but we also have central heating and broadband.'

'The old and the new together,' said Rose. 'No wonder you like it.'

'So you can tell your family it exists,' he said.

'They'll be so jealous when they see what I'm involved with.'

'There's no more paperwork to do here. I'll have to go back to England with you,'said Major Trent. 'We can avoid all the bother of exchange rates if we conclude our business in the UK. I think we deserve a special dinner, don't you?'

'Oh, Henry, let me rest this afternoon. I'd like to look at the village and perhaps get some gifts to take back.'

'Righto – see you in the entrance hall at seven. That's still early for Italy but at least we'll be sure of a table.'

* * *

Rose took her purple dress off the hanger. Major Trent had seen it before but she had so few opportunities to wear it.

She had a crystal necklace she wanted to put with it tonight, and some fresh make-up for her eyes – something she never usually wore.

What on earth am I trying to do? she asked herself. He already says he likes me. How much more do I want?

I'm just a silly old fool. It's time I got used to the idea that the world can go on very well without me. What do they say? Live every day as if it's your last. Is that what I'm doing? Well, if it is, then the condemned woman is going to have a very special last meal!

'I won't have that spaghetti thing for starters,' she told Henry when they sat down in the restaurant. 'It fills me up so I can't enjoy the rest of the meal. I'd like the risotto. I feel like prawns – followed by the fruit salad and ice cream, please, and then coffee and those delicious little biscuits.'

'No meringue?'

'It's not on the menu – unless I've missed it.'

'Raspberry pavlova,' he answered.

'Oh, I didn't see that. Thanks, Henry. That would be special.'

'I think I'll join you. How about a Rosé wine? It always makes me think of you.'

'That would be lovely. You spoil me.'

'There's no food quite like this in England.'

'If there is, I bet it's expensive.'

'You get what you pay for,' said Major Trent.

'I realise that, but I still can't believe a whole castle out here costs less than a three bedroomed house in London.'

'It's fate, Rose. Fate has brought us together and given us this fantastic opportunity. You have no regrets? It's not too late to pull out?'

'Regrets? Not now I've seen it. I'm itching to come on one of your courses.'

'For you it would be free. I'm sure you'd be an asset to the place.'

'You'd have me doing the washing up, I suppose!' She couldn't help laughing out loud at his face until he realised she was joking.

After two glasses of wine it occurred to her she was talking too much but she was having such a good time she didn't care.

They walked back to the farmhouse hand in hand and Henry pulled her to him and gave her a lingering kiss before wishing her goodnight and disappearing into his room.

She felt light-headed and sorry to be going home. Italy was such a magical place. Sussex would seem dull in comparison.

Major Trent drove her from the airport to her flat but said he would not come in.

'You'll need some time with your family,' he said. 'I'll see you on Tuesday. We can have lunch together before I go down to Cornwall.'

'I forgot that's where you usually are this month,' said Rose. 'Thanks, Henry. I've got so much to tell them.'

Somehow, she thought, I've got to break it to them that I'm going to give him twenty thousand pounds.

Chantelle seemed to understand but Katie was outraged.

'It's not me I'm thinking about,' she said. 'I don't want you to get cheated out of your savings.'

'I won't,' said Rose. 'I've been to the castle. I've seen all the particulars. You know there are Brits that do writing, painting and cookery courses at places like that. It's a wonderful opportunity. Daniel would love it.'

'Then let Daniel put money in,' snapped Katie.

'I'm doing it even if you don't agree,' said Rose, stubbornly.

'Then promise me one thing. Give him half the money first and see if he disappears with it. If he doesn't and I'm proved wrong you can give him the rest.'

'He did say he'd got until September to find it,' said Rose. 'OK. That's what I'll do if it will make you happy.'

'Not happy – but not quite so unhappy. Chantelle is bringing Daniel to lunch on Sunday. I suppose you are busy with your boyfriend.'

'No I'm not. He's off to Cornwall at the weekend. I'd love to come to lunch. I've lots of photos to show you all.'

Tuesday saw Henry and Rose enjoying a light lunch at the café on the pier. As soon as they had finished eating Rose said, 'Henry, I have decided to write you a cheque. Would that be acceptable?'

'A cheque would be fine - to my personal account, H.O.Trent.'

'I have something to tell you, Henry.'

'Oh yes? You've blown it all on the horses?'

'No. My daughter suggested I split the amount and give you half this month and half next.'

'She doesn't trust me.'

'She's just looking out for me. I'm sorry, it wasn't my idea.'

'That's all right. I understand. It must seem a lot of money to part with all at once.'

Embarrassed, Rose took out her cheque book and wrote the cheque, making sure she signed it. She wouldn't want him to have to return it because she had forgotten.

'I told Chantelle about the castle,' she said, handing it to him, 'and she and Daniel want to visit as soon as possible.'

'I'd love to have them. We should be opening in the spring. They could be our first guests.'

Thank goodness, thought Rose, he doesn't seem upset. Katie made me feel awful.

Daniel picked Chantelle and Rose up on Sunday morning and drove them to the Meadows. Rose was loaded down with gifts and the prints of her photographs.

It was after lunch, when they were seated in the lounge, that Daniel dropped his bombshell.

'Rose, I hate to say this but I'm not sure about Major Trent.'

'Now what!' she exclaimed. 'First Katie and then you. What have you found out?'

'It's not him. It's his sister. I looked up Celia Stone on the internet and she has a website. She looks nothing like the lady Henry introduced us to. That isn't Celia Stone.'

'And if it isn't Celia Stone who's to say Major Trent is Major Trent!' said Katie.

'He must be,' said Rose. 'I made the cheque out to Henry Trent. There's got to be a mistake.'

'Then he's nothing to do with Riverbridge Properties,' said Daniel.

'You mean- he doesn't own those hotels?'

'Right. He was just staying there.'

'But he told me he owned them all,' said Rose. 'He must have done. He was so at home there. The staff all treated him as if he was someone special. You saw him, Daniel. He was so friendly and polite. There's no way he could have been a fraud. There must be another explanation.'

'Yes, he fooled me, too, Rose,' said Daniel, 'but I'm afraid it's true.'

'It's a pretty elaborate scam,' said Chantelle. 'Weren't you a tiny bit suspicious?'

'Wait a minute,' said Rose. 'There was something a bit fishy about the hotel in Malta.'

'What was that?'

'He never appeared for breakfast. You know, I don't think he was sleeping there. How could he treat me like that!'

'That proves it,' said Daniel. 'How much did you give him, Rose?'

'Ten thousand pounds. Is there time to stop the cheque?'

'What day was it?'

'Tuesday.'

'We'll try first thing tomorrow.'

'But what if he's genuine?'

'We tell the police and Trading Standards. If there's another explanation they'll find it. It's a pity we don't know what he looks like.'

'We do. I have photos.'

'If they can catch him in Cornwall we're laughing.'

'If he is in Cornwall,' said Chantelle. 'If he's as clever as he seems he won't even be there.'

'And I did so like the castle,' mused Rose.

'There must be at least three of them in it,' said Daniel. 'You've had a lucky escape, Rose.'

'I feel a complete fool. I'll find the photo,' and she took out a thick envelope and sorted through the pictures until she found it.

'I'll ring the hotel in Cornwall and find out if he's there,' said Daniel. 'That won't make him suspicious. I could pretend it's for a honeymoon.'

Chantelle blushed. 'Don't say that.'

'Why not – we'll have one, won't we?'

'Who said we were getting married?'

'Well, we are, aren't we?'

'I haven't been asked yet. I might say no.'

'Why?'

'Just to be awkward,' said Rose. 'She's always said she doesn't believe in it.'

'Don't you?' said Daniel, staring at Chantelle.

'We've never discussed it,' snapped Chantelle, 'and now is not the time.'

'I'm sorry. I didn't mean...' He looked crestfallen.

'Let's get this sorted first,' said Katie, 'and worry about other things later.'

So Daniel rang the hotel to find that Major Trent was not there and had not made a booking that year. A call to Blackpool confirmed that the Major was not there either and was not one of the owners of the establishment.

'We'll ring the police,' said Katie. 'They don't have weekends off. They'll come round.'

At eight that evening she was proved right. The doorbell rang and she opened it to two detectives.

'You rang the station, Mrs Longman?' asked the smaller of the two. 'I'm Detective Constable Peters and this is my colleague, D.C. Grove. May we come in?'

'Yes, of course. Thank goodness you're here. I think tomorrow might be too late.'

'You are concerned about a Major Trent?'

'Yes, do sit down. Daniel can tell you all about it. This is Rose, my mother and Chantelle, her companion.'

'Daniel?' said the detective.

'Daniel Curtis,' said Daniel. 'I'm a friend of the family and I've met Major Trent.'

'We've got a photo,' said Rose, holding it out to the policeman.

'Thank you. Yes, that's the bloke. What has he done?'

'We aren't sure,' began Rose, 'but we think he's got away with ten thousand pounds.'

'He tricked Rose into paying for a hotel in Italy. He says he's the director of a firm called Riverbridge Properties but I don't think that's true,' said Daniel.

'Where's the hotel, Rose?' asked the detective.

'In Tuscany. I went out there to see it. It's a castle. Everything seemed to be above board.'

'And what made you suspect him, Mr Curtis?'

'We met someone he said was his sister in Cornwall and called her Celia Stone, but she wasn't. I looked on line for directors of Riverbridge Properties and Celia Stone looked completely different.'

Daniel was breathless with talking too fast.

'When did you give him ten thousand pounds, Rose?'

'On Tuesday. I wrote a cheque. We were going to ask the bank to stop it tomorrow. How could I have been so stupid?'

'And do you know where Major Trent is now?'

'No. He's disappeared.'

'Again.' He looked at his colleague.

'Major Henry Osborne Trent, as he calls himself isn't really a Major. He was a captain in the T.A.

The London police have a file on him as a fraudster but haven't been able to catch him. He doesn't always use the same deception. Last time it was selling insurance. His sister, Cheryl Trent, helps him. They're pretty clever, but this time we might be able to stop them. If they've gone abroad it's going to be tricky. Our best bet is the money. We'll come to the bank with you tomorrow. If it's too late to stop the cheque they might allow us to trace it. Which is your bank?'

Rose told them and they left after making an appointment to meet at ten o'clock the next day.

'I'd better take both of you home,' said Daniel. 'You will let me know what happens, won't you?'

'It's a good job the shop doesn't open on Mondays,' said Chantelle. 'I'd never be able to concentrate.'

'I don't know how I'll be able to wait until tomorrow,' said Rose, as she collapsed on to sofa in their flat. 'I feel all wound up. I never though anything like this could happen to me.'

The manager of the bank was apologetic but the money had been paid out in cash.

'Can you tell us where?' asked the detective.

'Certainly – our branch in Shoreham.'

'That's it,' shouted Rose. 'That's where he'll be – on the boat!'

'He has a boat?'

'Yes, on the river. He said it belonged to a friend but I bet it's his.'

'Well, if he has a boat he's probably long gone. I'll alert the lifeboat station and send an officer to join them. If you show us where he's moored we may have him.'

Chantelle watched Rose climb into the police car and speed away.

Once again the police had featured in her life. She'd still had not heard about the people who had attacked her in the Lake District. She supposed they had got away with it. And now Rose had been defrauded. Why couldn't their lives be simple and crime free? Her mind was in a turmoil. She felt left out. She needed to call Daniel but was reluctant to do so. Had that been a peculiar proposal, last night? If it was, what was her response?

After all those years with James and no ring on her finger should she abandon her principles and marry Daniel? How much did it matter to him?

'Chantelle Curtis,' she muttered. She didn't like it. It wasn't her. One marriage should be enough for anyone, she thought. I just hope I don't lose him altogether when I tell him.

'The Beach side of the river?' asked the detective as the car raced towards Shoreham.

'Yes, there are other boats there that look as if people live in them all the time.'

'We know it.'

But when they reached the mooring the boat had gone.

The car radio crackled and the driver answered it.

'They've got them,' he said, with a big grin on his face. 'The lifeboat caught them before they'd got out of the estuary. They're bringing them back.'

'Both of them?'

'Yes, him and his sister. Twenty minutes later and they'd have been out in the channel and away.'

'Thank goodness,' said Rose. 'I feel sick.'

'Get out, walk about. Well done, Mrs Smith.'

Rose stood, looking at the river. The tide was out and there were stretches of mud on either side. It wasn't a beautiful view. There were factory buildings on the other bank. She took a deep breath and let it out slowly.

So Major Trent had never been the owner of Riverbridge Properties. He'd just been staying there, like a spider in a web, waiting for a gullible victim and she'd been the fly.

He'd been clever. She might have suspected him if he'd been alone but once he had introduced her to his sister and Daniel had been satisfied they were genuine she had not only believed him, but liked him enough to want to have him in her life.

I should be grateful for all I have, she thought - my health, my friends and my family. What more should anyone want?

CHAPTER

SIXTEEN

Next day Rose had a call from Katie.

'Robbie's coming home,' she said. 'Not to stay, just to bring his fiancée. Isn't it exciting?'

'I do hope we like her,' replied Rose.

But there was only one room free in Katie's house. Now here was a dilemma. She couldn't ask Robbie straight out whether they were sharing a bed, not over the internet. What was she to do?

Chantelle had the answer. She and Rose were at the Meadows for Sunday lunch.

'Put a single bed in with the double bed and let them choose.'

'It will be like condoning pre-marital sex.'

'No, it won't. It's facing reality. It's that or asking him. Isn't that right, Rose?'

'I don't like it,' said Rose, 'but times have changed.'

'Mr and Mrs Thompson had specified two singles

when they booked. They can't be moved to a double. Miss Porter has the little room with the single bed. She's booked for a month. I can't shift her. There's only the big room with the double bed.'

'That's the family room, isn't it? What's in there now?'

'A cot,' said Katie.

'Haven't you got another single bed?'

'Yes, downstairs. It's a sofa bed. The one Heather used when she was injured.'

'Well, get that upstairs, make it up and give them the choice.'

Robbie and Sharon rang Katie from Heathrow.

'We're here, Mum,' said Robbie. 'We've got a room in London for the night. We'll come down by train tomorrow. Can you pick us up from the station?'

'Of course. That was very sensible. Call me when you're on the train.'

'There,' she told Bernard. 'He said 'a room.' I bet they share a bed.'

Bernard didn't reply. It didn't matter to him what the young people did. He was just pleased he was going to see his son again. It was all right being surrounded by women most of the time but he felt a special connection to Robbie. He had been slow to develop, like his father, but without his hearing problems.

Watching him grow into a confident young man had been one of the greatest pleasures of Bernard's life.

He hoped he would like this young woman that Robbie had chosen to be his wife. She would have to be very understanding to be a partner to his only son.

He need not have worried. Sharon was unlike anyone that they might have imagined.

Firstly, she arrived in a pair of thick jeans and a leather bomber jacket.

Then, her red hair glowed at them from under a woollen beret. Her hazel eyes twinkled as she shook Katie's hand, and nearly broke her fingers.

This was a girl who looked as if she belonged in the outback, a girl who was probably more at home on a horse than in a car.

She helped Robbie haul their cases into the boot of Katie's car and jumped into the back, hugging her haversack.

Robbie gave his mother a quick kiss and sat down beside her.

'This is grand, Mrs Longman,' said Sharon.

'Call me Katie,' she replied as they set off, 'everybody does.'

'Sure thing, Katie,' came the confident reply.

Robbie was grinning widely and Katie suspected that he knew Sharon would be a surprise. She hoped that, under her brash, almost masculine, exterior was a kind and gentle heart. She trusted her son's instincts about animals, even human ones.

Katie had been nearer the truth with her guesses than she could have supposed.

Sharon was, indeed, a horsewoman. She was so experienced that she was taking part in trials for the Olympics.

'Do you think Sharon will be able to get a ride at the stables?' asked Robbie.

'I'm sure she will,' said Katie. 'I don't suppose you could get Robbie on a horse?'

'On the contrary, Katie,' she replied. 'Robbie is a fine rider. He's got his own horse back home. Didn't he tell you?'

'No, he didn't. How many more secrets, Robbie?'

'Plenty,' said Robbie. 'What you don't know won't hurt you.'

My, thought Katie, You've changed.

Seeing the two of them together reminded Katie of how she and Bernard had been when they were in love.

To outsiders she must have seemed bossy but there was an understanding between them that meant, while allowing her to take the lead in most situations, Bernard would make certain that he agreed with what she suggested and, if not, insist she accept his decision. On all important matters she told him the options and they decided what to do together.

It seemed Robbie and Sharon had a similar understanding. Much of what they did appeared to be without discussion, as if each knew what the other wanted without asking.

'When are you planning on getting married?' she asked Robbie, on one of the rare occasions she had him to herself.

'It depends on the Olympics,' he explained. 'If Sharon is chosen we'll wait until after them, so it won't be for a couple of years, but if she isn't it could be next year. Could you come out, Mum?'

'I don't know. I wouldn't want to come without your father. I'd need to know because of the business. People book one year for the next.'

'How long are you going to go on doing the chiropody, Mum?'

'As long as I can. I might stop if your grandmother came to live with us but now she's in the flat with Chantelle. That doesn't seem likely.'

'Dad should be retiring soon.'

'They'll keep him on as long as he's useful. He loves it there. I wouldn't want him to stop.'

They were interrupted by a call from Heather. Katie left them to chat to each other. She would ask her daughter another time if she could bring the baby down to see them. It hurt that Rose had seen her but she had not. She was hoping they would come in the summer holidays.

From what she overheard Robbie was planning to visit Heather and when he ended his call she asked how he intended to spend his time in England.

'We want to go to as many places as possible,' he said. 'It might be the only chance Sharon gets to see this country. I'm taking her to Bath, and then over to Wales. If we come back to you for a weekend I want to go up to Yorkshire and Heather would like us to go and see them. Two weeks isn't really long enough. I'm just glad Sharon isn't the kind of girl who wants to go shopping in London.'

'Doesn't she want to see the sights?'

'Not really. We bought some postcards and if there's time we might fit in the Tower of London. We're both happier out in the country, Mum.'

'So you're hiring a car?'

'Sure thing. We couldn't do all that on public transport.'

She should be grateful he had come back at all, she thought, but there wasn't much time to get to know her future daughter-in-law.

Robbie's visit was over all too quickly and she thought life would return to normal until the news came that the Major was to be tried the following month and Rose would be the main witness.

Rose paused on the steps of the court. She had both Daniel and Katie with her for support and the prosecuting lawyer had gone over her submission with her.

'Just tell the truth,' everyone said, but she was afraid of making a mistake when she was asked questions. 'Take your time,' was the advice. 'Don't let them rush you.'

How would she feel when she saw Major Trent again? What would the jury think of her? She had to wait in another room while Katie went into the court room.

'I'm with you, Rose,' said Daniel, reassuringly.

Katie watched the prosecutor rise and accept the judge's invitation to begin.

'I will show how the supposed Major Trent targeted Mrs Rose Smith when she went on holiday to Blackpool,' he began. 'He befriended her, invited her to dinner, giving the impression that he was not only the owner of that hotel, but also of one in Cornwall and one in Malta.

When he discovered Mrs Smith was planning to go to Cornwall he booked himself into the same hotel and also invited her to the one in Malta.

To ensure that neither she, nor a friend, discovered his deception, he invited his sister to stay at the hotel for one night, naming her as Celia Stone, a director of Riverbridge Properties, the real owners of all three hotels.

In Malta he ensured she had an enjoyable holiday and came to trust him.

He then informed Mrs Smith that he needed money for the purchase of another property, in Italy.

When Mrs Smith showed an interest he invited her to visit this castle and see for herself what a good investment it would be.

Impressed by the castle, Mrs Smith offered him twenty thousand pounds.

However, family members suggested she pay Major Trent ten thousand pounds and reserve the rest until she was certain it was a viable proposition.

Having given Major Trent a cheque for ten thousand pounds Mrs Smith was informed by Daniel Curtis, who had been in Cornwall with them, that the Celia Stone they had met was not the Celia Stone who was the director of Riverbridge Properties.

Understanding this to be the case, Mrs Smith then tried to stop the cheque but it had been cashed and Major Trent and his sister were on board his boat on the way to Europe. Fortunately the police managed to stop them before they got away with the money.'

Then it was Rose's turn to give evidence. She took the stand and recited the oath. Her eyes were fixed on the lawyer.

'You are Rose Smith, of 27a, Southway Parade?'

'I am.'

'And did you meet Major Trent in Blackpool? What made you think he was the owner of the hotel?'

'I didn't at first. Then I asked him outright and he said yes. He knew the chef and what meals to order. He seemed very at home in the place. He said he spent four months there every year and I had no reason to doubt him.'

'Then he said he'd meet you in Cornwall?'

'Yes, he said he'd come back early from his hotel in Malta and stay with me for a few days. I was on a coach trip.'

'And did he tell you he owned this hotel, too?'

'He'd already said so. When he introduced us to his sister and said she was Celia Stone my friend Daniel looked on line and found that was the name of a director of the company.'

'Riverbridge Properties?'

'Yes, that seemed to clinch things.'

'So you went to Malta?'

'Yes, Major Trent showed me all over the island.'

'But there was something unusual about this holiday, wasn't there, Mrs. Smith?'

'Yes, but I didn't realise it at the time. Major Trent not only never came to breakfast, he also refused to dine at the hotel. He said they had been inspected and had failed and so took me out for meals.'

'And you believed him?'

'I did then. Now I wonder if he was staying at that hotel at all.'

'And you believed him when he told you about the castle in Italy?'

'Yes, there were pictures on line. It looked beautiful but he said he couldn't find all the money in time.'

'So you offered him twenty thousand pounds?'

'He said that was how much he needed – but I wouldn't have given it to him if I hadn't seen the castle.'

'And you did?'

'Yes, I paid for myself to go out there for a couple of days. It was very impressive.'

'So, when you returned you gave him the money?'

'Not all of it, my daughter suggested I gave him half so I made out a cheque for ten thousand pounds.'

'And then what happened?'

'Daniel, the man who had been on holiday with us in Cornwall looked for Celia Stone on the computer and found she looked nothing like the woman Henry had introduced us to.'

'So Major Trent's sister had nothing to do with Riverbridge Properties?'

'That's right, and if she didn't, he didn't, so we tried to stop the cheque.'

'But it was too late.'

'Yes, they had a boat in Shoreham. Luckily the police arrested them before they got very far.'

'And they still had the money?'

'Yes, I believe so.'

'Thank you, Mrs Smith.' said the judge. 'Have you any other witnesses, Mr Frazer?'

'Yes, my lord, Mr Daniel Curtis.'

'Well, I think this is an appropriate time to stop for lunch. We will continue at two pm.'

Rose stumbled as she left the witness box. She could feel her heart hammering in her chest. She knew Daniel would corroborate all she had said, but she was afraid. She still had the defence lawyer to cope with. She had to find somewhere to sit down.

Katie found her sitting by the front entrance and took her for a cup of tea and a sandwich. 'I'll be in there all afternoon,' she said. 'You should be in the waiting area, not by yourself in the cold.'

'You'll find me, and tell me what is happening?' asked Rose.

'Of course, if I'm allowed. Let's go and find Daniel.'

Katie listened eagerly to Daniel's evidence, backing up everything Rose had said. He fielded the questions from the defence, insisting that Major Trent had told them he owned all three hotels and even bought some photographs which his sister said was for advertising.

Next it was time for Rose to face the opposition. She stepped into the witness box, trying not to look as if she was staring at the jury. She could only really see the front six. There was a nervous looking young woman, a man with a turban, a middle aged woman, a thin young man in a suit and tie and an older man, dressed casually in a check shirt and body warmer. She couldn't imagine any of them feeling especially sympathetic.

'Do you mind telling the court your age, Mrs Smith?' asked the lawyer.

'I'm seventy six.'

'And the holiday in Blackpool – was it something you often did?'

'No. I'd been in Wales for some years but I felt like doing something different.'

'You were a widow ready for an adventure?'

'I suppose so.'

'And when you met Major Trent, what did you think?'

'I don't know what you mean.'

'Did you like him?'

'I suppose so. He seemed like a gentleman.'

'And a wealthy one?'

'I suppose so.'

'So when he began to discuss the hotel with you you assumed he must be connected. Is that right?'

'Not without reason. I asked him.'

'Did you ask if he was connected to Riverbridge Properties?'

'Not in so many words.'

'But later he showed you his card, isn't that right?'

'Yes"

'And did it say Riverbridge Properties?'

'No. It said Holidays of Distinction.'

'So you had no proof that he had any connection to the hotel except that he was staying there?'

'No – but that was in Cornwall. It was different there.'

'How was that?'

'He introduced me to his sister.'

'Cheryl Trent.'

'Yes, but he called her Celia Stone.'

'Really? We checked with reception and she booked in as Cheryl Trent.'

'But that's what he said, ask Daniel, he was there.'

'We will, Mrs Smith, but couldn't it be that you were mistaken?'

'No. I remember. I just assumed his sister was, or had been, married to a Mr Stone.'

'And you remember the holiday in Malta?'

'Yes.'

'That Major Trent was generous enough to pay for?'

'Yes.'

'And he took you out and treated you to meals. That isn't the actions of someone who wanted to defraud you, is it?'

Rose couldn't answer. It had felt so romantic, if a little rushed, at the time.

'I don't know. I only know he didn't seem to be staying at the hotel.'

'Which proves, does it not, that he has nothing to do with Riverbridge Properties?'

'I don't know. I'm getting confused. Could I have a drink of water?'

After a short pause the lawyer continued.

'Nearly done, Mrs Smith. About the castle in Italy. You saw pictures online?'

'Yes, we downloaded them. It looked beautiful.'

'It was fully furnished?'

'Yes.'

'And you understood it was for sale?'

'Yes.'

'So you took the sensible precaution of going to view it?'

'Yes.'

'But didn't Major Trent say it was occupied?'

'Yes – he said the owners were abroad.'

'And you saw the sale particulars?'

'The agent had them.'

'And do you know the name of this agent?'

'No. I left all that to Major Trent.'

'I put it to you, Mrs Smith, Major Trent was showing you the type of castle he hoped to purchase, not the actual building, but you misunderstood.'

'It didn't seem like that.'

'So you offered him money?'

'Yes.'

'He didn't ask for it?'

'Not directly. He just told me how much he needed.'

'And you were happy to supply that, no strings attached?'

'I thought I'd be involved. He said he was going to have a cookery school.'

'That sounds a little far fetched, if you don't mind me saying so. What qualifications did he have for that, I wonder?'

'He seemed to know a lot about food.'

'He seems to have impressed you with his knowledge, anyway.' The lawyer smiled as if he was pleased with his little joke.

Rose blushed. She felt the eyes of the jurors on her. What were they thinking-that she was a silly old fool that had become enamoured of a rich gentleman and was trying to back out of an arrangement?

'I'm sorry,' she said, looking at the judge in despair. 'I don't know what to say.'

'The money,' prompted the lawyer. 'This ten thousand pounds that you gave Major Trent. Why wasn't it twenty thousand as agreed?'

'My daughter said not to trust him.'

'Your daughter. You trusted him but your daughter didn't. So on your daughter's say so you tried to stop the cheque. Had Major Trent done anything to cause that?'

'He lied about his sister.'

'But we have no proof of that, Mrs Smith. In fact, we have no proof of anything you claim. Major Trent is the innocent party in all this. You owe him an apology.'

'Apology!' spluttered Rose. 'Never. I know when someone is trying to cheat me. It might have taken me a long time but I know he's guilty.'

'Please sit down, Mrs Smith,' said the judge. 'We need to hear from other witnesses.'

It was a tired Rose who went back to the flat to tell Chantelle what had happened.

'Did you think the jury believed you?' she asked.

'I don't know. At least there are two of us telling the same story. I'd be lost without Daniel.'

Next day the defence began by giving a short speech about Major Trent's activities with the T.A. He told how he had worked his way up from being a porter in a hotel to helping in the kitchens and how, being unable to buy a home of his own, he took to living in hotels. His sister, Cheryl, had a flat in London which he sometimes used as a base.

Major Trent was then called to give his account of the events already mentioned.

He told how he had befriended Rose and, when she expressed a desire to go abroad, suggested Malta. He booked her into another Riverbridge Properties hotel because he thought she would find it more familiar.

The castle in Italy had been a dream of his for some time and he and his sister intended to retire there but the one pictured was just an example of the kind of place they would like, not the actual building they intended to buy.

The twenty thousand pounds offered by Rose was an investment, intended to provide a little extra income for her, but not substantial enough, he thought, to be concerned about and was surprised when she limited the cheque to ten thousand pounds, although he was happy to wait for the rest.

'My client pleads not guilty,' he said. 'It is all a misunderstanding. At no time did he ever claim to be the owner of the hotels. He did not request money from Mrs Smith. In fact, he advised her not to invest if she was concerned about the viability of the project. He and his sister owned the boat and used it to cross over to France. They were doing that when they were stopped by the police. There was no intention to defraud. On the contrary, my client is very fond of Rose Smith and is sorry she misunderstood the situation.'

I wish she could hear this, thought Katie. It's a pack of lies, but very convincing.

When the defence called Cheryl Trent, Katie wondered if this really was the person Rose had described to her.

Her dark eyes were hidden behind thick rimmed spectacles but her long black hair fell, smooth and long, onto her slim shoulders.

She looks like Wonder Woman in disguise, thought Katie, glamour pretending to be plain or a scheming witch trying to look innocent.

Cheryl answered the defence lawyer's questions with a soft, clear voice, confirming her stay at the hotel and insisting she was introduced to Daniel and Rose as Cheryl Trent.

The defence then called the manager of the hotel in Blackpool.

He answered proudly that Major Trent had stayed with them for the four months of the Christmas lights for three years.

'He was a welcome and perceptive visitor,' he said. 'We have never had a suggestion of anything untoward in his behaviour. We always tried to make his stay as comfortable as possible and appreciated his recommendations, especially regarding the menu.'

Katie's heart sank. Major Trent was beginning to sound like the perfect guest.

The defence next called a passenger from the coach in Cornwall and she told the court how they had witnessed Rose and Major Trent embracing.

Katie began to get angry. It might seem as if this undermined Rose's case but it didn't. It just showed how far under Major Trent's spell she had been.

However, the image of her mother in Major Trent's arms stayed with her after the witness had left the box and she had the horrible feeling that it had been imprinted on the memories of the jury, too.

They'd seen Rose – didn't they realise her kindness was being exploited? What more did they have to do to make her evidence more convincing?

The fact that the prosecution had ended the day before with witness statements from the bank, about the cheque and the police about the chase, meant Rose's testimony could easily have been forgotten. They would be reminded, of course, but it wasn't the same. They would have gone home with their heads full of facts not considerations of motive. Even she had been left with one abiding image, Rose, in Major Trent's arms.

When the prosecution lawyer began to question him she was even more concerned.

'Mr. Trent,' said the lawyer, 'You call yourself Major but you were not in the regular army, were you?'

'No, I was in the Territorials – but I rose to Captain and have every right to use the title Major.'

'And isn't it true that at the time you met Mrs Smith in Blackpool you told her you were the owner of that hotel?'

'I did meet the lady, yes, but I did not tell her I owned the hotel. I have no connection to Riverbridge Properties.'

'But you did suggest you meet up in Cornwall?'

'I did say I was staying there. Once again, I'm sorry if she got the impression I was the owner.'

'You also met Mr Curtis?'

'Yes.'

'And he believed you were the owner of the hotels?'

'I don't know what he believed. He did say he'd like to take some pictures of the place.'

'And then you invited Mrs Smith to your hotel in Malta?'

'Not My hotel, an hotel. She had never been abroad and I knew the area.'

'So you paid for a holiday for her out of the goodness of your heart?'

'I object,' said the defence lawyer.

'No matter,' said Major Trent. 'I will admit I had grown very fond of the lady.'

'So fond that you felt you could ask her for money for your hotel in Italy?'

'I didn't ask. She offered. I told her I was setting up a consortium and she could buy a share.'

'To the tune of twenty thousand pounds?'

'Yes. She wanted to be involved. She came out to Italy.'

'But you hadn't found a castle?'

'No, but I knew one that looked just how I wanted ours to look.'

'And did she realise that?'

'I hoped so.'

'Well, it seems otherwise, doesn't it, Mr Trent?'

Sitting outside the court Rose felt herself shaking. Why wouldn't people believe her?

Katie and Daniel came to join her. 'The judge has made up his mind,' said Daniel.

'It's not up to him' said Katie, 'and the police know the Major's a crook. It's a pity we aren't allowed to tell the jury.'

'If there's any doubt they have to find him innocent,' said Rose. 'What did it seem like, Katie?'

'I'm not sure. There's still the closing speeches. It's your word against Major Trent's.'

CHAPTER

SEVENTEEN

Nothing new emerged from the closing remarks and the jury were sent away to deliberate.

Two hours later they were back, with the foreman declaring that they were unanimous that Major Trent was innocent.

The verdict had a disastrous effect on Rose. When she heard she collapsed, gasping for breath and holding her chest.

'Quick,' said Katie, 'Call an ambulance. I think she's had a heart attack.'

They didn't wait to see a jubilant Henry Trent come out of the court, only to be put in handcuffs by the police again. He was read his rights and whisked off in a police van to London. He had more questions to answer.

Rose was rushed into intensive care and Daniel and Katie told to go home and call in the morning.

'There's nothing we can do,' said Daniel. 'She's in the best place.'

'That wretched man. He nearly killed her,' Katie said. 'I can't understand why they didn't see what kind of man he was.'

'He was certainly clever,' said Daniel. 'He'd put nothing on paper. He'd relied on her being gullible.'

'I wonder how many other people he's done it to,' said Katie. 'I hope he rots in hell.'

'He'll get his comeuppance,' said Daniel. 'Are you OK to drive home?'

'Yes, thanks, Daniel. I need to tell everyone else. You go and see Chantelle. She'll need your support.'

'I expect she'll want to visit tomorrow.'

'They usually say only family,' muttered Katie, 'but she's as much family as any of us. Poor Mum.'

'Don't panic. If they thought she was in danger they wouldn't have sent us home.'

'There's that, I suppose. See you tomorrow, Daniel. Thanks for your help.'

The police told her, the following week, that Major Trent was back in custody and, this time, unlikely to get away with his crime.

'It's a different charge,' said the detective. 'He befriended an elderly widow who had a number of valuable antiques. He pretended to be a dealer and took some away to examine. He left a receipt with a false name and address.

He sold the antiques to a fence but we were watching the shop for another case and when we interviewed him he told us about the Major. He wasn't the Major, then. He called himself Gordon Wear.'

'Trent? Wear? He liked his rivers, didn't he?'

'Anyway, the fence gave us a good description and is ready to cooperate. When we realised Gordon Wear and Major Trent were the same man we picked him up after your trial. He's with the Met. He won't get away this time.'

'And his sister?'

'We suspect she does all the planning and designed the leaflet. The police are searching her flat. If she's left anything behind, they'll find it.'

'Ten thousand pounds wasn't a lot to be running away with.'

'No. We think they've been defrauding people for years, with different aliases. They were only using their real names now as it was the final scam in this country.'

'You know Rose collapsed after the trial?'

'Yes, I'm sorry. How's she doing?'

'She's out of ICU. She's on the ward. I don't think she'll ever be the same.'

'Well, thank her again and let her know about the Major. It might cheer her up.'

It wasn't cheering up Rose needed so much as an answer to the question that had been disturbing her. How could she go back to the flat?

Whatever the doctor said she knew she could no longer spend time and energy going up and down those stairs. She needed to be living on ground level. She wished, now, that she had done what she originally planned and bought a bungalow.

She didn't want to go into a care home. She couldn't stay at Katie's. All the bedrooms were upstairs.

She was frightened to get out of bed and go to the toilet by herself in case she fell. She felt she had aged ten years and spent many a night sobbing silently to herself.

When the doctor told her she was well enough to be moved Katie brought her some outdoor clothes and she dressed slowly. Then she watched Bernard wheel a chair to the side of the bed.

'Do I have to go in that?' she grumbled.

'We're up two floors,' said Katie. 'We've got to go in the lift.'

'Where are you taking me?'

'I told you, we've got it all arranged.'

'I don't like surprises.'

'You'll like this one.'

While Rose was in hospital Katie, Chantelle and Daniel had racked their brains to find a solution to her residential problem.

'She can't walk very far,' said Katie. 'But she'll get better. She's lost confidence.'

'It's a pity she sold the mobile home,' said Chantelle.

'I think I know someone who could help,' said Bernard. They turned towards him. Nobody had realised he was listening. They hadn't seen him sitting in the corner, listening to their conversation.

'Who, Ned?' said Katie.

'Joe, at the bowling club. His brother works at Eastleigh, in the depot.'

'The train depot?'

'Yes, at the works. He says they are selling off some old carriages. He was going to buy one to be a garden shed.'

'Train carriages!' exclaimed Daniel. 'They make restaurants and homes out of them. It would be the perfect solution. You could put it in the garden. There's plenty of room.'

'Wouldn't it need a lot of work?' asked Katie, dubiously.

'Maybe, but it's worth a try. How do we get hold of Joe, Bernard?'

So Bernard told them and they decided to club together to buy a train carriage for Rose.

Once it was converted, Daniel and Chantelle both had a hand in the decoration. Some of Rose's belongings from the flat were moved into the carriage, which now had a kitchen and toilet. There would be no need for Rose to use the facilities in Katie's house if she did not wish to.

The inside was painted a pale green with floor and curtains a soft brown. On the walls, in between the many little windows, were a couple of Daniel's photographs, two seascapes, one with seagulls and one with starlings.

The varnished wooden fittings gleamed and, best of all, there was only one step up to the carriage door.

Rose had a walking frame from the hospital and looked worried as they exited the car.

'Have you turned one of your downstairs rooms into a room for me?' she asked.

'No, Mum. Wait and see. We have to go round the back,' Katie replied.

Slowly the little group trooped behind the garage into the rear garden. Daniel held back to let Rose see what they had done.

'Goodness!' she exclaimed. 'Is that for me?'

'Yes' said Katie, 'and we've got a ramp if you need it. You don't have to struggle up the step.'

'Can we go inside?'

'Of course. I hope you like it. Daniel and Chantelle did all the decorating.'

Rose's face was a picture. For the first time in weeks she was beaming. There was a handle by the door and she grabbed it eagerly, abandoning her walker and leaning forward to see inside.

'Katie. It's wonderful!' she declared. 'Look, my own kitchen, oh, good heavens, Daniel's pictures, a dining room, a bedroom, a shower, I can't believe it!'

'Then you like it, Mum?' said Katie, following her inside.

'Like it? Of course I don't like it - I love it. Oh my, I don't deserve this.'

She was getting flushed and her breathing was speeding up.

'Sit down, Mum,' said Katie, severely. 'You're too excited.'

'Do you blame me? This is so wonderful. How much did it cost? I must pay for it.'

'We could always charge you rent,' said Katie.

'Yes, yes, what a good idea.'

'Nonsense, Mum. I was joking. You'll still have expenses. We can discuss that later, but, if you like it, this is your new home.'

'But Chantelle?' said Rose, sitting herself down on the padded bench seat. 'What about her? She needs help.'

'And she'll get it. Daniel is going to help out. He's not going to live there but he's insisting on helping with the rent.'

'And the charity don't mind?'

'It's nothing to do with them. The place is in Chantelle's name. They don't need to know where the money comes from as long as she pays on time.'

'I've let them down, haven't I?'

'Not at all. You helped them come to an arrangement that suits them both. It's all turned out for the best, Mum.'

Katie's wishes came true when Ryan and Heather brought little Karen to stay in the summer holidays. She had left a week free in August, with no other guests in the house, so that she could spend as much time with her granddaughter as possible.

There wasn't much they could do with a one year old but they took her to the beach where Rose said she would sit on the pier and watch them as she could not walk easily over pebbles.

They had fish and chips in a café near the front with Karen sat in a high chair, munching a rusk.

Katie peeled some of the batter away from the fish and mashed up a little of the white flesh with some milk and offered it on a spoon to her daughter.

It wasn't something Rose would have done although, in her day, they never went out for a meal with a young child.

To everyone's surprise the baby seemed to like it.

'I didn't know she'd be a fish eater,' said Ryan. 'That will give her good strong bones.'

'Like her mum,' said Rose. 'Perhaps she'll be an athlete one day.'

'She's already big for her age,' said Katie, 'and we are going to take her swimming when the school holidays are over and there's more room in the pool.'

''Lisa's pool?'

'It has to be, doesn't it? There's one nearer but we promised that we'd let her other Grannie have the pleasure of watching her.'

'Did you ever find out what happened to Major Trent, Katie?' asked Ryan.

'Yes, he got six years. Apparently he asked for some other swindles to be taken into consideration.'

'But not Rose's?'

'No – he got away with that, and his sister got away with everything. They didn't have enough evidence to convict her.'

'So you never got your money back, Nan?'

'No,' said Rose. 'It was a harsh lesson.'

That evening she sat in her train carriage home, content in the knowledge that her family were safe and happy.

She had given up working in the shop. Instead she had gone back to making jams and chutneys as she had done when she was a young married woman.

She'd even asked Katie if they could have a few chickens. She knew Bernard would enjoy building them a shed and a run.

She was back where she belonged, in a country cottage on the Downs, and she had another task to look forward to.

Katie was going to leave her in charge of the B and B while she and Bernard went to Australia for Robbie's wedding.

It would be autumn, and they only had two visitors booked in, but she was pleased her daughter thought she was well enough to cope.

It was nice to be trusted, and nice to have her life back on track.

If you enjoyed this story why not try Julie C. Round's other novels?

LANE'S END
A man with learning difficulties has to find a new home and forge a new life for himself after the death of his mother - but can he succeed in the modern world?

UN-STABLE LANE
A family fight to save their smallholding when floods threaten to destroy their home on the South Downs - and who is the curious stranger?

THE THIRD LANE
A teenage girl has to make difficult decisions about her career and love life when her circumstances change - and what draws her grandmother to Wales?

NEVER RUN AWAY
A married woman tries to adopt a new identity when she leaves her husband for life in a mysterious house in a south coast town - but how does he react?

NEVER PRETEND.
A single mother marries a schoolteacher who has difficulty accepting her son for adoption - and who commits the eventual crime?

A LESSON FOR THE TEACHER
Three young women leave college in the 1960's thinking they have little to learn but soon find they are very ignorant about men. Will they ever find true love?

www.juliecround.co.uk